"A Rebel, a Maverick, an Adventurer, a Gypsy—

I'll bet if you'd been born a boy you'd have stowed away years ago on a freighter bound for Hong Kong." His eyes twinkled.

"Don't, Thane," she pleaded.

"Okay. You win this time, Les. But you can't chase unicorns forever."

"There's nothing wrong with dreams!" she said. Tears filled her eyes.

"Dreams can be pretty lonely company on a cold mountain night," he said. His tone was mocking.

CATHRYN LADAME
is as young and romantic as her own heroines. She has admitted that her heroes are based on real characters but suggests that it is up to her readers to identify them.

Dear Reader:

I'd like to take this opportunity to thank you for all your support and encouragement of Silhouette Romances.

Many of you write in regularly, telling us what you like best about Silhouette, which authors are your favorites. This is a tremendous help to us as we strive to publish the best contemporary romances possible.

All the romances from Silhouette Books are for you, so enjoy this book and the many stories to come. I hope you'll continue to share your thoughts with us, and invite you to write to us at the address below:

Karen Solem
Editor-in-Chief
Silhouette Books
P.O. Box 769
New York, N.Y. 10019

CATHRYN LADAME
Trail of the Unicorn

Silhouette 🦢 *Romance*

Published by Silhouette Books New York

America's Publisher of Contemporary Romance

Other Silhouette Books by Cathryn LaDame

Winter's Heart

SILHOUETTE BOOKS, a Simon & Schuster Division of
GULF & WESTERN CORPORATION
1230 Avenue of the Americas, New York, N.Y. 10020

Copyright © 1983 by Cathryn LaDame

Distributed by Pocket Books

All rights reserved, including the right to reproduce
this book or portions thereof in any form whatsoever.
For information address Silhouette Books, 1230
Avenue of the Americas, New York, N.Y. 10020

ISBN: 0-671-57209-1

First Silhouette Books printing March, 1983

10 9 8 7 6 5 4 3 2 1

All of the characters in this book are fictitious. Any resemblance to actual persons, living or dead, is purely coincidental.

Map by Ray Lundgren

SILHOUETTE, SILHOUETTE ROMANCE and colophon are
registered trademarks of Simon & Schuster.

America's Publisher of Contemporary Romance

Printed in the U.S.A.

To all those I love
and have loved
who share the search
for the bright and shining dream . . .

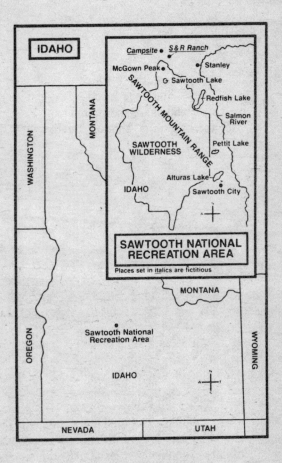

IDAHO

Campsite • *S&R Ranch*

McGown Peak •
• Stanley

Sawtooth Lake

Redfish Lake

Salmon River

SAWTOOTH MOUNTAIN RANGE

SAWTOOTH WILDERNESS

Pettit Lake

Alturas Lake
Sawtooth City

IDAHO

SAWTOOTH NATIONAL RECREATION AREA

Places set in italics are fictitious

MONTANA

WASHINGTON

MONTANA

OREGON

Sawtooth National Recreation Area

IDAHO

WYOMING

NEVADA   UTAH

Chapter One

"Miss Lesley, it's nearly nine," the gray-haired woman in the housekeeper's uniform called up the stairway. Just as she'd expected, she was answered by a wail from two flights up.

"It can't be! On, no, I'm late!" came the agitated voice of a young woman.

Humming and shaking her head, Harriet resumed her dusting. She had just finished the living room and moved into the dining room when a whirlwind came flying down the stairs and passed her, heading for the kitchen, which was another flight down in the narrow town house.

"Morning, Harry. You're a doll for waking me. Wait till I see Uncle Graham . . ." Lesley dropped her purse and yellow linen suit jacket on the counter and poured herself a glass of grapefruit juice.

Harriet followed, clicking her tongue disapprovingly. "Sit down now, miss, like a proper civilized lady, and I'll have you some decent food in no time."

Sniffing ruefully at the lingering odor of fried bacon from Uncle Graham's breakfast, Lesley declined. "Great idea, Harry, but that's exactly what I have—no time." Lesley laughed at her own joke. Despite her objection to the younger woman's cavalier attitude toward nutrition, Harriet had to laugh, too. Even though Lesley had lived there for only the past year, the veteran housekeeper felt as though she'd raised her. The combination of shiny long black hair, sparkling blue eyes, and a warm and giving nature had wormed her way into Harriet's heart.

After gulping down the tart juice, Lesley gathered her briefcase and purse and jacket and started out, calling a cheery good-bye to Harriet, who shouted in answer, "Don't you be tellin' Mr. Graham I woke you, now. He left strict orders that you were to have a good sleep!"

"Your secret is safe with me, Harry!" Lesley shouted back as she shut the ornate midnight blue front door behind her. Her smile deepened as she pictured Harriet's "tsk-tsking."

The stately residential street was fairly

quiet at this hour of the morning, with no taxis in sight. Frowning at the time on her wristwatch, Lesley started for the corner, where a waiting cab could usually be found.

"Just as well," she mumbled to herself. Although she managed to affect the air of a self-assured young career woman, at home in New York City, to herself she admitted the truth: hailing taxis was torture. Perhaps it was her lack of height or her dislike of making a public spectacle of herself by waving her arms, whistling, or using one of the other spells and incantations the natives practiced to achieve their objective.

Finally settled in a cab, Lesley gave the address of the Unicorn Society Institute, the world-famous ecology organization, where she worked as personal assistant in public relations for her uncle, Graham Chadwick, the founder and president.

During the relatively short ride, Lesley marshaled her arguments for her confrontation with her uncle. For a year now, since her graduation from college, she'd worked successfully with him, taking much of the burden of meetings with Institute board members and sponsors off his shoulders, already overloaded with administrative responsibilities.

"It's poetic justice," he would lament, resting his hand on yet another pile of folders, reports on whale populations, on pending environmental legislation, on an expedition monitoring volcanic activity in Alaska and the American Northwest, on a myriad of other topics, all requiring his personal attention. "One of the reasons I founded the Institute was that I felt other such organizations were bogged down by paper work. Twenty years later I find myself in exactly the same predicament."

Because she dearly loved and admired him and the work toward a better world done at Unicorn, Lesley had been proud to do her share.

Now, however, she was determined to do more. Feeling that she had a good background in the day-to-day goings on in the magnificent old building, international headquarters for the Unicorn Society, she now readied herself to insist that she be given a field assignment. Biologists, anthropologists, botanists, archaeologists, oceanographers, geologists—all these specialists were scattered throughout the world, feeding data back to her uncle and his staff of communications experts in New York. They, in turn, produced the award-winning studies for various governments and the books and documentaries on ecological matters for movies and television that had made the Institute famous.

And Lesley Wallis, she thought, condemning herself, sits in elegant restaurants sipping wine and entertaining people, "selling" them on Unicorn, even though they don't know a cactus from a penguin. She sighed. Almost all the people she met in the course of her job were interesting and pleasant, but she was beginning to feel stale. As sponsors or directors of Unicorn, they asked her questions about current projects. Part of her job was to be up to date on the latest expeditions and achievements of the field teams, so she always had answers, but she was tired of mere words.

If only I could experience what field teams experience, she thought, thrill to the diversity of this world, test my own strength and endurance, make some contribution to human knowledge . . .

"Miss . . . hey, lady, you're here . . ." the driver was saying, bringing her out of her reverie.

"Sorry." Lesley smiled, saw to the fare, and left the cab to make her way across the crowded sidewalk. When she entered the elegant old building, she stopped in front of the bronze plaque affixed to the wall near the door.

THE UNICORN SOCIETY INSTITUTE

In this building men and women will gather together united in their desire to understand and to preserve the natural wonders of this world, and the mythical perfection of the unicorn will symbolize their quest.

GRAHAM CHADWICK
Founder and President
April 13, 1960

Feeling the familiar stab of pride the words always caused, Lesley made her way through the crowds of tourists already filling the lobby. Just before she reached the elevator, a teenaged girl stopped her.

"Excuse me, ma'am, but could you tell me when the first tour starts?"

Lesley consulted her watch. "In just about ten minutes," she answered. "Which tour are you taking?"

"Golly! You mean there's more than one?"

Lesley smiled kindly at her, remembering her own bewilderment the first time she'd visited the bustling institute. "Just two. The first is quite long, encompassing all the exhibits with a special stop for a film in the Unicorn Gallery. The second tour is shorter—just a general walk-through. Got that?"

"Whew! Thanks a lot—there's no time for us to take the long one. We've got to meet my grandparents for an early lunch, and, well . . . thanks again!" she called, dashing back to join her family with the information.

Stepping into the carpeted elevator and pressing the button for the eighth floor, Lesley sighed to herself. During all the years she and her mother had struggled to make ends meet after her father had died, she had never dreamed that such an exciting life would be hers. Uncle Graham had often pleaded with his sister to allow him to help her, but Jean Wallis had had too much pride for that. Not until her own illness threatened Lesley's chances for a college education had she capitulated. At least Mom's last years were comfortable, Lesley had told herself again and again. Well, financially secure, anyway, she amended. From the day Bill Wallis had died, when Lesley was just twelve, Jean had never been a well or a happy woman. The couple had shared a very special love, one that Lesley had hopes of finding for herself—someday.

"But not yet—my life is just right the way it is now," she murmured as she stepped off the elevator. "If I can just convince Uncle Graham to let me try my wings."

Humming, Lesley entered the main office section, done in muted shades of green and gold and boasting, as did each floor of the Institute, an extensive array of wildlife and scenic prints. "Morning, Mrs. Crandall," she greeted the stern secretary.

A frown was her answer. "Why, Miss Wallis, your uncle told me not to expect you until at least noon." Graham Chadwick's word was law to Mrs. Crandall—deviations from it were not to be tolerated.

"I'm sure he did," Lesley replied, laughing. "And I'll have something to say about that later." She picked up her mail, sorting through it absently.

"You were out late last night, weren't you,

with the Cardozas and the Bergstroms?" the secretary persisted.

Lesley nodded. "But so was Uncle Graham, and he was here before you as usual, right?"

"Well, yes, I suppose so. I don't know where that man gets his energy," Mrs. Crandall clucked, patting an imaginary stray hair into place.

"From leading an exemplary life," said Graham Chadwick, standing in the doorway to his office.

Lesley smiled, walking toward her tall uncle. "Good morning, Uncle Graham." She kissed his cheek. From the way his eyes sparkled it was obvious that he was fond of his niece.

"Are you busy right now?" Lesley asked, peering around him to see if there was anyone in the office.

"Not at all. Come in, my dear," he invited. She preceded him into the large room, resplendent with Oriental rugs, sculptures of various animals, including the unicorn, of course, and paintings and photographs of the many lands visited by Institute expeditions.

When she was settled in a chair, he took his place behind the massive antique oak desk. "What can I do for you this morning, Lesley?"

"It's not what you can do for me, Uncle Graham," she began in a very exaggerated public relations voice, "but what I can do for you."

"Really, Lesley, I can almost see the cigar waggling at the corner of your mouth. Are you trying to sell me something?" He leaned back, relaxed but wary, sure that his bright young assistant had something on her mind that he wasn't going to like. Lesley saw the suspicion building in the wise blue eyes.

"I'm trying to sell me," she said flatly.

"Why, I am sold on you, my dear. You have become invaluable to me and to the Institute. Just last night Enrique Cardoza said . . ."

"Thank you, Uncle Graham," she interrupted. "But I wasn't speaking of my PR duties. I want to become more involved in the day-to-day work of the Institute."

"Day to day?"

"Out there," she said, gesturing broadly. "There's so much to see, to know, to do, and I want to be a part of it."

Graham smiled a trifle sadly. "Youthful enthusiasm. I had almost forgotten what it's like to desire grand adventures."

"Nonsense, Uncle Graham—you're barely fifty . . . all right, barely fifty-six—and how many people of any age would have gone back in a shark cage the way you did just two years ago?"

"But, Lesley . . ." he began, then was interrupted as an uncharacteristically emotional Mrs. Crandall burst into the office without warning. For an instant the shock of her behavior rendered both Lesley and her uncle speechless.

Breathlessly, the secretary announced, "Mr. Chadwick! It's Thane—I mean, Mr. Fraser—he's here, coming up now! The doorman, from downstairs, at the door, he called —oh, sir, Mr. Fraser!"

Having imparted this bit of news, Mrs. Crandall flew out of the office as abruptly as she'd entered it, slamming the door behind her. Seeing the broad grin on Graham's face and the suggestion of moisture in his eyes, Lesley asked, "Who is this . . . Thane somebody or other? What's hap . . ."

Coming around his desk, her uncle opened the connecting door between her office and his. "Excuse me for a moment, my dear? It is very important."

Automatically doing as she was asked, Lesley was halfway through the door before she thought to question her polite but firm dismissal. "Who is . . ."

"Thank you, Lesley," Graham said, firmly closing the door in her face.

Lesley scarcely had time to reach her cluttered desk before she heard her uncle's booming laugh, a sound reserved for very special occasions. His greeting was answered by a deep, low voice, definitely male. Slightly miffed at her dismissal, both for personal and professional reasons, Lesley couldn't resist hovering near the door.

"We have missed you, my boy, this past year. Why haven't we heard from you?" Graham was saying.

"The corporation was in worse shape than I'd thought, Graham," answered his guest. "But it looks as though things here have managed to stumble along without me," he continued, and Lesley could almost see the smile on his face.

Lesley walked to her desk and sat down, idly drumming a pencil on a pile of folders. "Uncle Graham can have the wonderful Thane," she muttered, opening the top folder and beginning her morning's work, already delayed by her lateness and Mr. Fraser's ill-timed visit. The first folder contained a request for Unicorn's aid in a project to investigate the destruction of farmland for industrial purposes. Knowing Graham's interest in the problem, she wrote a rough draft of a press release on the proposed project and tagged both it and the folder for Graham. Next she read a heartening report on the increasing population of alligators in the American Southeast. With a satisfied smile, Lesley typed a press release and sent a note to the managing editor of Unicorn Watch, the bimonthly newsletter sent to all society members worldwide, to feature this item in the upcoming issue. In the world of diminishing wildlife, good news was altogether too infrequent on her desk.

After a while, she halted her furious pace and admitted to herself that she was still brooding over events in Graham's office. She realized that the bad timing could hardly be faulted to Mr. Fraser. Nevertheless, because of him she would have to begin all over again convincing her uncle to send her on a field study. It hardly endeared Thane Fraser to her. And if she were truthful, Lesley would have to admit that until the unknown Mr. Fraser's arrival no one else had ever claimed such obvious affection from her uncle. She couldn't help feeling an ignoble jealousy.

While Lesley worked, unable to hear the conversation between the two men, her uncle's thoughts, too, were on her request. Thane's return after a year's absence seemed heaven-sent to Graham, but he kept his ideas to himself until he got some answers from his visitor.

"Tell me, Thane, how is everything? Especially your dear mother—how is she?" There was intense concern in Graham's voice, which Thane noted but forebore commenting on.

"Mother is doing beautifully. It was difficult at first—she and Dad were very close, you know."

Graham nodded, a reminiscent look in his eyes.

Thane continued, "She's planning to live in New York City now."

"Lydia—here in the city! Why didn't you call me? I could have . . ."

"Relax, Graham. I've arranged for my place to be completely redone and she'll live there with me for a while. She intends to call you when she's settled. It'll be a week or two."

Graham smiled, caught himself, and asked, "And the company?"

"In capable hands. It should keep Mother secure."

"What about you, Thane?" Graham asked.

Thane rose and walked to the large windows with their panoramic view of the city. Graham watched him, unused to seeing the Institute's brightest light in such formal attire as dark gray suit, vest, and tie. During the nearly ten years that Thane had worked under the auspices of Unicorn, he could most often be found in denims, khaki, or diving gear. Even when he was in New York, briefing the Institute's writers and researchers on his latest findings, Thane had seldom dressed the part of the young executive he was, both in his late father's Canadian business and at Unicorn.

Running long fingers through thick, wavy dark hair, Thane turned to the older man—his mentor, his companion, his friend. "Any openings at Unicorn?" he asked, smiling.

Graham leaped up, embracing the tall young man who had become more than a son to him. "Thane! You know you'll always . . ." he began before moaning softly and sliding back into his chair with Thane's help.

"Graham—what is it?"

Breathing shallowly and keeping his eyes closed, Graham whispered, "Please, some water. It's nothing. I'm all right." Beads of perspiration on his pale face belied his words.

Moments later, watching Graham sip at the water he'd brought, Thane asked, "Have you seen Bailey recently?"

Graham waved off the question as he regained his normally ruddy color. "That old mother hen—I haven't time to spend hours taking his foolish tests. Ever since you left the Institute, I've just been too busy."

"Don't try to make me feel guilty, Graham. Any number of people would have leaped at the chance to direct field studies. You just try to do too much. Coordinating expeditions, supervising research, communications, public relations—why didn't you fill my job?" he scolded, a worried frown on his face. In the field and in the city Thane had watched Graham Chadwick perform extraordinary feats of endurance and courage. It was somehow unbelievable and more than a little frightening to see him weakened.

"As a matter of fact, I did fill one of those jobs—at least in part. I have my own personal assistant who handles the bulk of the public relations around here," Graham defended himself, gesturing toward the closed door to Lesley's domain.

"I suppose that means you also filled my old office," Thane said.

"Only because I had bigger plans for you, Thane. Am I to assume you're back to stay now?"

Thane nodded, grinning.

"What would you think of Antonelli's office?" Graham asked, pleased to see the interest spark on Thane's face. "He left the Institute about three months ago, and the rooms are still empty. I knew you'd come back someday, my boy."

"I don't know what to say, Graham, except thank you." He looked thoughtfully at the older man. "Let me call Dr. Bailey?"

"Nonsense."

"You know I will whether you agree or not."

"I forgot how damnably take-charge you can be, Thane. All right, I'll call him—tomorrow—I promise," Graham conceded.

"Mrs. Crandall will call him—today," Thane insisted.

"I give up. Between you and Lesley, a man isn't allowed a thought of his own," Graham complained.

"Lesley?"

"My personal assistant—came soon after you left. I'm really anxious for you two to meet."

"What's wrong with right now? I'm in no hurry—if that's all right with you?"

Graham grinned widely, punched a button on the intercom. "Lesley, will you join us, please?"

Thane sat down again, saying, "I'm anxious to meet the man who managed to wrest some responsibility from you, Graham."

Lesley had come through the door behind him as he spoke. "It wasn't all that difficult, Mr. Fraser. As for being a man—well, I'm sorry to disappoint you."

At the first sound of her voice, a surprised Thane turned to look at her, then rose from his chair.

His six feet of muscled leanness caused a strange feeling in Lesley's knees. She became even more businesslike.

Extending her hand, she walked toward him. "I'm Lesley Wallis, Mr. Fraser." Her tone was formally polite.

He took her small hand, holding it a trifle longer than was necessary. Smiling into her eyes, so that she couldn't avoid the glittering, dark depths of his gaze, he said, "I'm pleased to meet you, Lesley." Turning to Graham, he asked, "Wallis—wasn't that your sister's name?"

Graham nodded. "Lesley is my niece. She's been with me since Jean's death, and with the Institute since she graduated from college."

Finally releasing her hand, Thane indicated a chair next to him. Feeling like a guest in this office, which before Thane Fraser's entrance had been a second home to her, Lesley obeyed and sat down stiffly.

"This is going to sound like the oldest line in the book, but if you've been with Graham for the last few years, how did I miss you?" Thane asked.

Lesley smiled. "Uncle Graham insisted I finish school before I even got near the Institute. He always said he knew too many people who—how did you put it?" she asked her uncle.

Before he could answer, Thane recited, "People who went off in irresponsible directions in search of some harebrained adventure at the expense of their educations."

"Oh, you've heard the speech too?" Lesley asked, laughing at the nearly perfect mimicking of her uncle.

"Heard it! I'm the one he invented it for," Thane informed her.

"You don't appear to be any the worse for your decision," Lesley observed, studying his face. She noted the arched, thick brows over penetrating dark eyes, the slim, strong nose, the high cheekbones, the mobile, expressive mouth. His air of self-confidence told her that here was a man to be reckoned with. He lounged there totally at ease, yet even though his manner was relaxed and sociable, Lesley sensed something uncivilized about him, a leashed virility. In spite of herself she was fascinated by the way the skin around his eyes crinkled when he smiled, the result of long hours in the sun and wind.

Aware of her close inspection of him, Thane grinned mockingly at her and teased, "Well, Miss Wallis, have I passed inspection?"

Lesley could feel her cheeks grow warm as her hands gripped the soft leather of the chair arms. She was conscious that her perusal of him hadn't been strictly for professional reasons. She was sure he'd already guessed that, but she refused to confirm his own inflated opinion of himself and his attractiveness. "I'm sure my opinion of you is of no concern to anyone," she said sharply.

"You underestimate yourself, Lesley," he said, grinning.

Coolly she directed her next question to her uncle, who had been observing their reaction to each other with interest. "I have a lot of work to catch up on, Uncle Graham. Will you excuse . . ."

"Humor me, dear, and stay a while. Thane and I might have something to say that would interest you." He earned a questioning look from both his listeners. "First of all, Lesley, Thane will be working with us from now on, as director of field studies and as an expedition head, when he chooses to be." Graham paused long enough to let her absorb this information. Lesley tried not to show her amazement in front of the two men. She thought that in one sentence Graham had virtually abdicated his role as active head of the Unicorn Society Institute—and to this smug stranger!

"But Uncle Graham . . ." she began, leaning forward in her agitation.

"It's the position he held before, Lesley," he

forestalled her. "You should be pleased— you're always after me to rest more."

This was true. Lesley swallowed her protest and her questions. Turning slightly in her chair to look at him, she said, "Well, welcome —uh—back, Mr. Fraser."

Chapter Two

"Thane—I insist, Lesley." Regarding her closely, Thane addressed her uncle. "Tell me, Graham, will I be entitled to an assistant, too?"

Graham laughed his booming laugh. Lesley got the definite impression that that joyous sound would be more common now that Thane Fraser was back. She was again more than a little jealous of this stranger's claim on her uncle's affections and trust. Since she'd been Graham's assistant, they had become a unit, interdependent, closed to outsiders. That situation, it seemed, was about to change. She wasn't at all sure it was a change for the better. This man disturbed her in ways she was ill-prepared to deal with.

"John Fillmore might be willing to take that

job," her uncle suggested with a serious face, barely able to hide his merriment. John Fillmore, as both Lesley and Thane knew, was a staff researcher, slow-moving and nearing sixty. Obviously, he was not what Thane had in mind. Lesley put a hand over her mouth to hide her grin of satisfaction.

"On second thought," Thane was saying, "I'll just stumble along on my own for now."

"I thought that's what you'd say," Graham said, grinning. "Speaking of which—are you still unattached, son?"

Thane looked at Lesley, who stared at her folded hands—folded to still their trembling at the turn events were taking. She didn't want to know anything personal about Thane Fraser—but that desire, too, was overridden by her uncle's question.

"Footloose and fancy free, Graham."

Obscurely, as though something was required from her, Lesley remarked, "Come now, Mr. Fraser, I can't believe you spend your evenings alone!"

"I merely said I was unattached. I never said I spent my evenings alone," he corrected, arching an eyebrow. "However, I haven't been to New York for almost a year. Would you be so kind as to help me fill one of my lonely evenings?" Thane asked, his tone ironic.

Lesley had never slapped anyone's face in her life. Suddenly she felt a strong urge to do just that to Thane Fraser. Why the man irritated her so, she couldn't have said, but being in the same room with him was becoming intolerable. She half rose to leave, with or without her uncle's permission, when Graham answered for her.

"Of course she will, Thane," he said, shocking her to her core. "As a matter of fact, you can be her escort to the Founders' Day Ball this Saturday." Seeing her shocked look, he added, "He'll make a much more presentable escort than your white-haired uncle, Lesley."

She sat down again. What could Uncle Graham be thinking of?

Thane was grinning at her helplessness as she stammered, "Really, Uncle Graham, I don't think . . ."

"It will be nice for you and Thane to get to know each other, dear. After all, you'll be working closely together," Graham argued.

"But . . . but . . . I'm *your* assistant, Uncle Graham. Why . . ."

"You've done such an excellent job, Lesley, and you know more about what's going on at the Institute than any of us. Thane will need someone to fill him in, and that someone is you," Graham answered. It sounded like a compliment, but Lesley knew her uncle well enough to recognize a direct order when she heard one. Argument was useless; she knew that, too.

"I'm no ogre, Lesley," Thane assured her.

Graham chuckled. "He's telling the truth, my dear. Every secretary he ever employed fell in love with him." Graham looked at

Thane. "No need to worry about those complications where Lesley is concerned though."

"Is that so?" Thane asked. Lesley refused to look at either of them. This conversation was becoming increasingly difficult.

"Totally career-minded is my Lesley," Graham sighed. "Oh, she has a busy social life, but it's all with ancient codgers like me, convincing them that Unicorn is the greatest boon to mankind since the wheel."

"Uncle Graham, please . . ."

"Don't be so modest, dear. It's the simple truth. An evening out with someone in your own generation is just what you need." Lesley shrugged her shoulders, aware that further protest was a waste of energy. "Don't look so condemned, my dear—I have more good news for you."

Steeling herself for yet another piece of Graham's news, Lesley waited quietly.

"Remember your request to go out in the field?"

Lesley nodded, feeling as though that conversation had been a thousand years ago.

"Thane has been living in concrete jungles for a year. As you and he will be working together anyway, what better solution than for Thane to take you on an expedition?"

"*What!*" Thane and Lesley shouted in unison.

Unruffled, Graham went on blithely. "I'm glad you both agree that it's a capital idea. You can probably be spared within a week,

Lesley, right after Founders' Day. Now, that's taken care of. Where are you staying, Thane?"

"At the Algonquin," Thane murmured automatically.

"You'll come stay at my home, of course," Graham said. "Just until things are straightened out for Lydia's arrival."

Lesley felt desperate for something to bring her back to reality. Thane Fraser, at Unicorn! Thane Fraser, in the field! Thane Fraser, in her home! She managed to ask in a choked voice, "Lydia?"

"Thane's mother," Graham answered. "A very, very dear friend. Why, I've known Lydia Emory—I mean, Fraser—since before she married André." His eyes softened. "Now, if you two will excuse me, I think I've done a fine morning's work. Perhaps I'll call Dr. Bailey now," he said to Thane, who nodded imperceptibly.

"Dr. Bailey—who's that? Is something wrong, Uncle Graham?" Lesley asked anxiously.

"Just a checkup, my dear. I've put it off too long," he reassured her.

Satisfied, Lesley rose. Thane did, too. "Well, good-bye, Mr. . . . uh, Thane."

"Not good-bye, Lesley. See you later," he said softly, taking her hand again.

Hurriedly, she withdrew it. She walked calmly to her office, though she wanted to run, and shut the door, resisting the irrational impulse to lock it against whatever it was out there that had upset her so strangely.

"Send your things over, Thane, and Harriet will have you settled by this evening, all right?"

Shaking Graham's hand, Thane nodded. "Kind of you, Graham. You know how I love Harry's cooking. It'll be a bit like old times—two crotchety bachelors trading stories all evening."

"Not quite. I neglected to tell you that Lesley lives with me."

Thane arched a brow. "Another reason to be pleased at your offer of hospitality. See you this evening, Graham." With the graceful and efficient movement that was his and his alone, Thane turned and left the office.

Graham sat down again, steepled his fingers under his chin, and murmured to himself, "I think I handled that rather well." Pleased with himself, he indulged in a bit of reminiscence of Lydia Emory, the girl he'd hoped to marry long ago. Unable to cope with his long absences and adventurous life-style, she had chosen André Fraser instead and gone away with him to Canada and a secure, settled life. Their son Thane had been born a year later.

When Thane had impulsively left college, signing on a Unicorn expedition vessel as a common seaman, Lydia had contacted Graham, asking him to watch over her son. Thane had soon proved to them all that he didn't need "looking after."

Within a few years he had worked his way steadily up in the organization until he had assumed responsibilities second only to Graham's own. After initial disapproval, André had accepted Thane's decision, even coming to boast of his son's achievements as honor followed award after award for his groundbreaking efforts and achievements. But upon the death of his father, Thane had been forced to return home to take care of his mother and take over the company reins.

But now, Graham told himself, Thane was back—the son who would have been his, the man who couldn't be a source of more pride and love to Graham than had he truly been his son. And Lesley was here, precious and beloved Lesley, his only family. Graham astounded himself at his planned interference in their lives, but he had already made up his mind that they must marry. Unlike the woman he'd loved, Lesley was knowledgeable about and a steadfast supporter of Unicorn and all it entailed, while Thane represented the best of Unicorn's present and future. It was all so eminently right, Graham assured himself.

Suddenly life was sweet indeed. And Lydia would soon arrive—gentle and tender Lydia, who shuddered at the idea of voyages to distant places and the hardships to be encountered there. But Graham had recently given up accompanying expeditions, making excuses to Lesley and others, secretly knowing it was because of his steadily deteriorating health.

My health! he thought ruefully. Nothing must interfere with the promising future he could now see. Sighing, he picked up the phone and dialed Dr. Bailey's number.

Lesley never knew how she managed to get through the rest of that day. Only the knowledge that the disturbing Thane Fraser had left the building enabled her to carry on with some semblance of calm.

When Mrs. Crandall looked at her with a question in her eyes, Lesley made some remark about being a little tired from the night before.

With Graham gone for the day to keep his doctor's appointment, Lesley found plenty to keep her busy. But the high spot of the afternoon came when a dozen long-stemmed red roses arrived from Mr. and Mrs. Cardoza, new Institute supporters whom she and her uncle had entertained the night before.

"Oh, Miss Wallis," enthused Mrs. Crandall, plunging her plain, squarish face deep among the buds and inhaling their sweetness with an audible intake of breath. "Aren't they gorgeous? You're so lucky!"

Handing her a rose for the bud vase on her desk, Lesley smiled. "I think I'll take these home to enjoy."

Mrs. Crandall glanced at the clock. "Almost time to leave," she sighed, again burying her nose in her flower and inhaling deeply. "Thank you for the rose, Miss Wallis, and good night."

"Night," Lesley called after her. She stood for a long time looking at the flowers in their long white box, willing herself to gather her things and start for home. Knowing that Thane Fraser would be there made leaving the office the most difficult thing she'd done all day.

Finally, she left, choosing in her preoccupied mood to walk slowly down the stairs, all eight flights of them, rather than take the elevator. She didn't even think about the roses she'd left on top of her filing cabinet.

The street had quieted down by the time she left the building, bidding good night to the night superintendent in the front lobby. She forced a smile when he remarked, "Guess things will be jumping around here again now that Mr. Fraser's back!"

It was a lovely summer evening. Before she found a cab, Lesley walked several blocks, deliberately choosing a street where bright red geraniums were blooming in large redwood tubs placed at intervals on the sidewalk. Just seeing the proof of summer amidst the skyscrapers soothed her.

When she reached her uncle's town house she unlocked the door slowly and walked inside. The living room was empty, but she must have made some noise, for her escape to her room, up two flights, was halted by her uncle's voice. It came from the den on the first floor.

"Lesley, is that you?"

"Yes, Uncle Graham." Inwardly, she sighed in defeat.

"Join us, please!"

Sighing, Lesley left her purse, briefcase, and jacket on the hall table. She straightened her slim yellow linen skirt and walked through the living room and tiny hall into the den. From the sounds coming from the floor below she could tell that Harriet was already busy in the kitchen. Perhaps, Lesley thought to herself, fate will be kind and dinner will be early tonight. Anything to cut short this dreaded evening!

Pausing a second at the door, she took a deep breath and went into the cozy dark-paneled room. Just as she'd suspected, there was her uncle, in his customary ancient leather chair, and there was Thane Fraser, lounging on the big, brown corduroy-covered sofa, exactly the spot that she usually occupied. Both men were holding tall, iced drinks in their hands.

Thane rose as she entered. "Good evening, Lesley." Lesley caught a mocking look in his eyes.

"We were just beginning to worry about you, dear. Was there some problem at the office?" Graham asked.

"No, no, nothing, Uncle Graham. I—well, I suppose I lost track of the time. Please forgive me, Mr. . . . uh, Thane," she replied, letting him know by the withering look she gave their guest that she could play the same game.

To her dismay, Thane came toward her, firmly gripped her elbow, and guided her to a place beside him on the couch. "Don't worry about it, Les," he said politely.

"Believe me, I won't," she whispered so that Graham couldn't hear. Again, she felt that quite irrational urge to smack his face. Somehow she resented his shortening of her name.

"What did you say, dear?" Graham asked.

"Lesley was just welcoming me, Graham," Thane answered for her. She tossed him a furious look.

"I'm so glad," Graham was saying. "It means a great deal to me that you two young people get to be friends." He paused, smiling. "Now, Lesley, how about a cool drink."

Sitting stiffly next to Thane, uncomfortably aware of the slight woodsy smell of his after-shave and of the pressure of his hard, long legs against hers, Lesley started to rise, saying, "Sounds wonderful, Uncle Graham. I'll get it."

A firm, long-fingered hand pulled her back down. "Allow me, Les. After all, you have been working all day." Again, he grinned at her, obviously enjoying her irritation. She started to protest, realized it was useless, and closed her mouth. A mutinous frown remained on her delicate features.

The balance of the evening was spent in the same frustrating manner. Thane had come to stay, and it looked as though he was determined to subvert Lesley's position in the household. Decisions and small jobs that had been her province were now delegated to Thane by mutual, unspoken consent of her uncle and an obviously smitten Harriet.

After dinner Lesley tried to excuse herself, pleading fatigue. Neither her uncle nor his guest would hear of it.

"Why don't you play for us, my dear?" Graham asked her, nodding toward the shining black baby grand piano sitting in the large front window alcove of the living room. It was a common request, as they often spent evenings at home in one of her small "concerts." But tonight!

"I'm not really in the mood, Uncle . . ." she started to say.

As usual, Thane was quicker than she. "If not for Graham, then for me, Lesley."

She frowned at him, but he continued. "Part of your duties as hostess?" he queried, putting her in an untenable position. To refuse now would be churlish. Thane had maneuvered her expertly. Lesley didn't think she would ever forgive him for the way he had commandeered both the Institute and her previously happy home.

Shrugging her shoulders in resignation, she

sat down at the piano, deliberated a moment, then began with a Schubert Impromptu followed by a Chopin nocturne. Her small audience applauded when she finished.

"Thank you, gentlemen. Now if you . . ."

Again she was forestalled, this time by her uncle. "One more, Lesley—my favorite, please?" He looked so relaxed and happy that she didn't have the heart to refuse.

Turning back to the keyboard, she began "La Vie en Rose." For a while she was lost in the music, playing simple variations on the main theme, variations that she'd improvised on previous occasions. So absorbed was she that she failed to notice Graham's inquiring look at Thane, which the younger man answered with a smile and a nod.

Suddenly her fingers froze on the keys. "Roses!" she exclaimed.

"What's wrong, dear?" Graham asked.

"Oh, I suppose it's not that important, Uncle Graham. It's just that the Cardozas sent flowers to the office, and I meant to bring them home. They'll be wilted by morning," she said rather wistfully. Sighing, she resumed her playing.

Graham interrupted her. "It's a shame to waste them, child. I'm sure Thane would be glad to drive you to fetch them."

Thane smiled. "Of course. I'll get my keys."

Horrified at the prospect of this errand with Thane Fraser, Lesley tried to wheedle her way out of it, but to no avail. Within minutes she was in his car, an elegantly European model.

Thane was his most charming self on the drive. Despite her earlier antagonism, even Lesley had to admit to herself that she was grateful for his company.

Chapter Three

When they were driving home, Lesley decided to show Thane her appreciation for accompanying her to get the flowers. "Thank you, Thane. I really would have hated to see these wilt away unappreciated."

"My pleasure, Lesley," he said softly, negotiating a turn.

Lesley could think of nothing more to say so she fell silent again and relaxed into the plush midnight blue upholstery. Arriving at the Chadwick town house, Thane pulled smoothly into a parking space directly in front. Lesley laughed.

"Does my parking amuse you?" he asked, smiling.

"Just that you've performed a miracle—

there's *never* a parking space here. It's one of the reasons we don't bother keeping a car."

His grin broadened. Lesley noticed that the tiny lines around his eyes deepened when he smiled. She brought herself back to reality just as he was saying, "I've always been lucky."

Somehow her awareness of him and his easy acceptance of his good fortune irked Lesley immeasurably. Everything, in her eyes, had come to him a bit too easily: looks, professional respect, charm, and now the Unicorn Institute. With a noncommittal sound, she hurried out of the car without his help and up the steps to the front door. Just as she was inserting her key, he came up behind her, so close that she could feel the warmth of him. Her fingers fumbled with the key and she couldn't get the door open.

"You forgot these again," he murmured near her ear. Turning slightly, Lesley realized he was carrying the large box of flowers, which she'd left in the back seat of his car. "Allow me," he said, and with a flick of his wrist, the door opened.

When they entered the foyer, she started to head up the stairs, but his voice stopped her. "Please, Les, join me in the living room for a minute. There's something I'd like to talk to you about."

Unable to think of a reasonable excuse, Lesley followed him in.

"Ah, there you be," Harriet exclaimed, coming up from the kitchen a second after Lesley had sat down on the gold brocade couch. "Mr. Graham has gone to his room, but he asked me to say good night and tend to these." She took the box of flowers from the chair where Thane had left them and bustled out.

"They'll be welcoming you in the morning!" she called over her shoulder. "Good night, both of you!"

They answered her, then stared at the fireplace until Harriet was well out of earshot. Lesley wished Thane would say whatever he had to say. She was increasingly edgy in his company and she heartily disliked the feeling.

Finally, when it seemed he was never going to speak, she turned to him and found him staring intently at her. "Well?" she asked sharply, unconsciously checking the buttons on her blouse. Honestly! The man was too blatant in his appraisal!

Without preamble, he announced flatly, "Going out in the field is not for you."

Momentarily taken aback, Lesley stared at him with anger and frustration sparking in her eyes. Thane's decision would be final on this matter, once he resumed his duties as director of field studies. Judging by what she'd observed today, she didn't for one minute think that even her uncle would dispute his right to destroy all her plans. Determined to remain calm, she prepared herself for a logical argument of her case.

He didn't give her the chance. In a calm voice he added, "You're far too delicate a woman to face the hardships of an expedition. I don't know what Graham could have in mind by his suggestion that I take you on one."

Her crushed hopes and his implied criticism of her uncle ignited the explosion.

"You . . . you chauvinist! How unreasonable! I thought thinking like yours went out in the nineteenth century. Uncle Graham, for your information, realizes that what I lack in muscle I make up for by willingness to learn and intelligence."

He smiled, infuriating her further. "What about Veronica Hastings?" she continued. "Mindy Smith-Collins, Angela Nomura? They're veterans of Unicorn expeditions—and Angela, at least, is smaller than I am!"

"But more experienced," he drawled.

Forcing herself to face him squarely, Lesley made her voice sweet and insinuating. "What kind of experience did you have in mind?"

She stepped back as he rose to stand, tall and implacable. In spite of herself, she was intimidated by his height, the breadth of his shoulders, and the sheer, maddening magnetism of the man. When his hands came on her shoulders, drawing her close to his smug, smiling face, she tried to twist away. Her efforts were useless against his strength. She was held as inexorably as if she were in a vise.

His face came nearer as he whispered, "I

meant in the field. Obviously, you meant this."

"No," Lesley moaned before his lips covered hers. At first, she pushed at his shoulders, but as his hands molded her soft curves to his hard leanness, she ceased to care about any experience but the one she was having. Her skin was alternately cold, then feverish, as his lips explored hers with casual expertise. The clean, rugged smell of him filled her nostrils.

Her reaction to Thane's kiss was startling and entirely unexpected. For long moments he savored her mouth, parted her lips, and took full advantage of her inability to resist him. Her arms circled his neck and she had to stand on tiptoe to caress his thick wavy hair. She found herself wishing the moment would go on and on, but he finally pulled away, leaving Lesley completely off balance.

Steadying her with hands on her shoulders, he laughed lightly as she stepped away. She couldn't look at him. Never in her few brief encounters with men had she known anything approaching this shattering response to a kiss.

"Well, well," he teased, "inexperienced but great promise."

At the end of her rope, Lesley snapped back loudly, "Not for you, you arrogant . . ."

She was silenced by his hand over her mouth. "Quiet—unless you want to disturb Graham or Harriet."

Lesley wrenched away from him, ran to the stairs, and was halfway up the first flight before she realized he was directly behind her. "Just where do you think you're going?" she hissed.

"I thought I'd go to bed," he answered calmly. "Now that the fire has died in the living room and you have left it."

"But . . . but . . . up here?"

By now they'd reached the landing outside Graham's room. The only other room on this floor was Graham's large study. Lesley lowered her voice even more.

Leaning close, Thane said softly, "Where else?"

Fuming with rage and frustration she started up the last flight of stairs. At the door of her room she turned, determined to see him securely behind his door before she opened hers. In the dim hall light his face was all planes and angles. It was all she could do to maintain an outward composure.

Hand on his doorknob, he said, "Besides, it's good practice."

All manner of disquieting possibilities entered her head. Forgetting to speak quietly, Lesley shouted, "Practice!"

Thane frowned at her, grabbed her wrist, and pulled her into his room. She was too shocked to protest. "Later this week or next we'll be sharing closer quarters."

"Are you crazy?"

He smiled, leaned on the doorjamb. "Not

really," he replied calmly. "Have you changed your mind about our joint expedition?"

He smiled at the swift incredulity on her face. "Thane! We're not going!"

"Why not?"

"I thought I was too delicate and too inexperienced."

"I've come to the conclusion that you're not as fragile as you look."

Against her better judgment, Lesley lowered her gaze to her feet and whispered, "And the inexperience?"

"Simple. I'll be your teacher." He tipped her chin up until he could look down directly into blue eyes that were growing wider by the second. Unable to challenge him—after all, she *was* inexperienced in outdoor skills, along with a few other things she preferred not to discuss—Lesley muttered, "Good night, Thane," and hurried from his room.

She spent the next few hours puzzling over his words and trying not to think of him, strong, warm, and compelling, in the next room. It wasn't the best prescription for a good night's sleep.

The morning wasn't any easier. Lesley overslept—another black mark against Thane Fraser as far as she was concerned—and not even the sight of her beautiful red roses, now in full bloom, at the breakfast table improved her mood.

Graham was seated across from Thane at

the sunny dining room with its view over the small walled garden. "Good morning, Lesley," he muttered, engrossed as always in the morning paper.

Lesley kissed his cheek. Her main concern at the moment was their guest. Unconsciously, she smoothed her plum-colored pleated skirt and adjusted the soft cowl neckline of her matching blouse. To her chagrin, Graham answered her unspoken question. "Thane waited for you, dear, but try to hurry, will you? There's a great deal I'd like to discuss with him at the office. He'll drive you in. See you later then."

Lesley grabbed his arm. "Oh, do you have to go ahead of us, Uncle Graham? I can get coffee and a roll at the Institute. Please, let me go with you."

"I wouldn't dream of it, dear. You young people take your time after all. I just remembered I have an early meeting with Ben Adams."

Lesley started to protest, but Graham was already collecting his battered briefcase, always overflowing with paperwork. It was the one disorganized area in his disciplined life. He headed out the door before she could argue. Lesley walked back to the dining room. She refused to meet the mocking dark stare of its sole occupant, eating one of Harry's ample breakfasts.

"Good try, Les," Thane murmured.

Lesley's gaze flew to him, angry and surprised. "I don't know what you mean," she insisted.

"Your escape attempt, of course," he replied mildly.

"You flatter yourself!"

Thane stood, took the few steps to her side, and smoothed a hand over her shining hair. "No, Lesley, you flatter me."

Lesley pushed his hand away just as Harriet came in carrying a tray of eggs, sausages, and fried potatoes. "Morning, Harry. That smells delicious, but I'm really not hungry—I'll just have juice."

Smiling, Thane resumed his seat near her. "And just what am I to do with all this food?" Harriet asked as she plunked the platter down in front of them.

Thane helped himself to more eggs and watched the two of them.

"Isn't it Wednesday, Harry?" Lesley countered, a knowing glint in her eye. She poured herself some juice and deigned to offer some to Thane, who nodded his acceptance.

Harriet shook her head in exasperation and blushed, then without another word whisked away the food platter and disappeared into the kitchen.

Thane sat back, bewildered. "What does Wednesday have to do with anything?"

Lesley smiled. "Today is the day Mr. Finnegan comes to collect the dry cleaning.

Harry always has a nice meal waiting for him, and they visit for a while. I discovered their little trysts my sophomore year in college, when I was home for a holiday. Uncle Graham still doesn't know." She hesitated a moment, concerned for Harriet's secret. "You won't tell him?"

Thane frowned at her. "For some reason, Miss Wallis, you have a very low opinion of me. Just to set your mind at rest, let me assure you that I wouldn't hurt or embarrass Harry for anything in the world. All right?" He stood up, towering over the seated Lesley.

Forcing herself to look up to him, she attempted an apology. "I was being unfair. I'm sorry, Thane," she said, ashamed at making her poor opinion of him so obvious.

"Forget it," he told her in a flat voice. "Are you ready to go?"

Without saying anything, she walked out of the dining room with Thane close behind her. "We're leaving, Harry! See you tonight!" she called down the stairs to the kitchen.

Outside the town house, Thane took her arm and helped her into his car. In the daylight she could see it was a long, low European make, obviously extremely expensive. It was one more reason for Lesley to chalk up mental black marks against him—she always thought that people who squandered their whole salaries on such luxury items were conceited and foolish.

They rode to work in silence. Well, she thought, silence is preferable to teasing flirtation.

At least she could deal with his silence. But the other—his closeness, his touch, his devastating kiss—left her confused and frightened and filled with the irrational fear that her sane, well-ordered life was about to end.

The next few days went by fast—too fast for Lesley. In spite of constant questioning from him, Thane refused to tell her exactly where they would be going.

"You're being very unprofessional," she complained one afternoon in his office.

"No matter. The trip isn't for strictly professional reasons, or even exactly for the Society at this point. I'm not even letting them pick up the tab. It's merely to get some fresh air for me after a year in cages—and to get experience for you, remember. You *do* still want that experience?" he asked, arching a brow at her.

Making a mental note to pay back every penny he spent on her, Lesley ignored him. "But the others . . ."

Abruptly, he cut her off. "Never mind the others. Now, where is the membership report for last year?"

Sighing, she dug through one of many piles of folders on his desk and handed him the one he'd requested.

It was like that all week. Endlessly, he probed, analyzed, discussed every facet of

Unicorn's operation. Lesley had thought she had an excellent grasp of the scope of the Society and the work at the Institute. Thane showed her how much she didn't know. They spent many hours digging through files of the past year's work in search of yet another answer to his questions.

Although he often commented on and once or twice even complimented her on her knowledge, Lesley felt as though she were sprinting just to keep up with his incessant inquiries. After a few days, she understood why her uncle placed implicit trust in Thane Fraser. He was brilliant, intuitive, creative, and quick, an original, with more knowledge in a hundred areas, it seemed, than some experts could claim in one. Whether checking over the budget, the appointment of board members, the deployment of field teams, the running of the laboratories, the public relations, the museum—or something as routine as the ordering of new cameras—he was thorough, concise, and clear. It was no wonder that the staff welcomed him back with open arms. One of them, Helga van Ernst, an obviously smitten middle-aged botanist, told Lesley that Thane was recognized internationally as an expert on endangered species in declining habitats. A small African nation had honored him three years before for his help in negotiating a kind of peaceful coexistence between elephant herds and native farmers.

All this astonished Lesley. When she had first met him, she had classified Thane as an overly charming dilettante who used his wits to scrape by. She soon discovered his authority was infinitely quiet, always understated, but absolute. He possessed an indolent grace and a way of relating to individuals that gave the impression that he had all the time in the world to listen, even if in reality he had at least twenty more things on his agenda before lunch. It was an indispensable gift for dealing with the many sensitive egos of the scientists and artists at the Institute. Grudgingly, Lesley admired him—at the office.

After several exhausting days, Lesley had to contend with him socially when he escorted her to the Founders' Day Ball, the first Saturday in July. She was determined to dazzle him, despite her antagonism.

She met him at the foot of the stairs. Her hair was upswept to give her added height and to emphasize the high, ruffled neck of the Victorian white lace blouse she wore. A lacy cummerbund showed off her waist, and the ruffle of her full black taffeta skirt rustled against the carpet.

"Well, it was worth it to have the bathroom commandeered for two hours," was his only comment.

Lesley wanted to throttle him, but instead she tilted her chin and walked to her uncle. "Lovely as a rose, my dear girl," Graham said as Lesley pirouetted before him.

"Aye, that she is," added Harriet, entering the hall.

"Not a rose, Graham—too civilized. Lesley intends to prove she's a bit more adventuresome, so . . ." Thane said. He handed her a small box of flowers, bowing slightly as he did so. Lesley turned her attention to his offering, hoping her eyes wouldn't betray her. He seemed taller and more startlingly handsome than usual in his tuxedo, and she was finding the fragrance of his after-shave very distracting.

She opened the box to find some tiny multicolored flowers. She looked at him, a question in her eyes.

"Wild flowers. I'm not sure they even have proper names. A botanist I know manages to grow them, as a hobby. They're quite a challenge."

Lesley sniffed their delicate fragrance. "They're enchanting, Thane. Thank you," she whispered, though she was still unable to meet his eyes.

"Let me help," he said as his strong fingers took the small corsage from her hands and fastened it at her waist. Such a casually intimate gesture caused her cheeks to turn pink, and she was grateful when Graham cleared his throat and announced that they must be leaving.

She was spared further comments as they hurried out to Thane's car. Lesley insisted that she, not Graham, sit in the cramped, tiny back seat. She took advantage of the twenty-minute drive to regain her composure.

As Graham's official hostess at this, her first Founders' Day Ball, Lesley spent the early part of the evening greeting guests. Even during the three-course dinner Lesley was preoccupied with her role. But when the small orchestra began playing the opening waltz, her misgivings about her escort returned full force. Thus far, only with the flowers had Thane claimed any rights as the "date" that Graham had arranged. Now, as she waited for her uncle to join her for the first dance, Lesley learned just how seriously Thane took his duties.

"Shall we?" asked Thane. He bent low so that she felt his breath on her ear.

Startled, Lesley stepped away. "What?"

"Dance. Shall we?" he repeated.

"Uncle Graham and I were to lead the dancing," she insisted.

"A pleasure he has delegated to me, Les," Thane reported. She detected triumph in his eyes.

Again Lesley started to step away, but his firm grip on her arm stopped her. He whispered, "Everyone is waiting—and watching, Lesley. Grow up and behave yourself."

Cheeks burning, she gave Thane a perfunctory smile and allowed him to take her in his arms. They glided into a flowing Viennese waltz. Lesley had never felt less graceful in her life. It was all she could do to remain stiff and unyielding in Thane's arms, when her senses were clamoring for her to melt against him. He guided her under the shimmering chandeliers, which bathed them in a romantic glow.

"It's a good thing I'm a good dancer, or we'd have crashed into a pillar by now," he muttered to her through a smile.

His ego was beyond belief! Still, Thane *was* a good dancer—excellent, in fact. He led her through the waltz with the same casual grace with which he did everything else.

Unable to fault him, unwilling to accept him as her treacherous senses wished, she forced herself to relax in his arms.

"Ummm, that's better," he said, grinning, as they whirled around the floor to the applause of the guests.

Smiling, Lesley said through clenched teeth, "I'm only doing this for Uncle Graham."

He arched an eyebrow, but she ignored him. When he stopped suddenly and invited their audience to join them, Lesley was forced to follow his lead. Within moments the dance floor was filled with other couples—men in formal black, ladies in chiffon and lace in myriad colors that became a blurred rainbow to Lesley's eyes. Taking advantage of the crush, Thane pulled Lesley closer as the waltz ended and another waltz, slower and more romantic, began. They slowed their steps.

"You look beautiful tonight," he said into her hair. Lesley fought to keep her equilibrium. She prayed he couldn't feel her pulses pounding.

"Thank you," she whispered.

His lips caressed her temple, then her cheek as he bent his head to her. They moved as one, the pressure of his taut thighs enflaming her until Lesley questioned her own sanity.

Just as the situation was becoming unbearable for her, she was rescued by Ben Adams, who tapped Thane lightly on the shoulder. "May I cut in?"

For just a second Lesley could have sworn Thane was about to refuse, and she steeled herself for a scene. Then he smiled, though it never quite reached his eyes, and graciously proffered her hand to the young man who waited.

As she began dancing with Ben, Lesley watched Thane's tall figure disappear into the swirling crowd.

"Did I make a mistake?" Ben was asking. Lesley turned her attention to him, realizing what she might be revealing by her actions.

"No, not at all," she hastened to reassure him. "I'm delighted to see you, Ben—somewhere other than on film!" Lesley did sincerely like the slightly stocky, round-faced Ben Adams. He was one of the Institute's underwater photographer/divers, and for a while, when he wasn't out on a project, she had dated him, cutting off that part of their relationship when Ben showed signs of becoming serious.

"Something tells me I'm too late to pick up where we left off," he sighed.

Lesley laughed, knowing that neither of them had ever been committed to the other. "It was never anything serious, and you know it, Ben!"

"Can't blame a guy for trying, Ms. Wallis!"

Lesley shook her head at him. They continued their dance in a spirit of lighthearted fun. Then she danced with her uncle, with several of the board members and sponsors, and with Ben again. She saw no sign of Thane, though she looked for him often. Each time she chided herself for her weakness.

Finally, toward the end of the ball she spotted Thane dancing with Eve Cortland, the young, glamorous wife of one of the Institute's oldest and most influential supporters. Mrs. Cortland was unashamedly clinging to her tall partner.

Lesley was incensed that Thane would jeopardize the whole Unicorn Society by his ridiculous behavior.

When she stiffened in his arms, her uncle asked, "Is something wrong, Lesley?"

Something in his voice made her suspicious. Darting a look at him, she found nothing more than innocent inquiry shining from his blue eyes.

"Nothing's wrong, Uncle Graham. I'm just a little tired, that's all." Against her will, her gaze found Thane whispering something in Eve Cortland's diamond-studded ear, something that caused the sleek redhead to giggle loudly. To Lesley's biased hearing, the irritating sound reverberated around the parquet floors and paneled walls.

"Must she always make an exhibition of herself?" Lesley hissed.

Graham looked at the woman in question. To Lesley's surprise, he smiled. "Why, they're just dancing, dear. Why are you so upset?"

"I am *not* upset. Thane Fraser can have all the Eve Cortlands in the universe, but must he parade his latest conquest here of all places?" Two bright spots of color appeared in her cheeks.

"Lesley, dear, you're overreacting. I'm sure . . ."

"Never mind, Uncle Graham, let's just get on with the evening." Lesley continued their dance, though she suddenly felt tired beyond belief. Why did the emotions she felt when she was around Thane always exhaust her, leaving her to feel as though she had been running a long, long time from something—or someone?

"Well, that's over for another year, thank heavens," Graham sighed. His face was pale and drawn with fatigue. "Thank you both for your help, and sleep well," he added, starting up the gold-carpeted stairs.

Lesley moved to follow him, but Thane stopped her. As they both watched Graham disappear into his room at the top of the stairs,

Thane said, "I may have been your escort, Les, but we never did get to dance more than once. Let's make up for that now." He started to lead her into the living room, where the light of a single small lamp lent a disturbing intimacy to the otherwise formal room. Lesley broke away from him.

"Let go of me, Thane—please! I just want to go to bed." She struggled against him, but to no avail. He was like pushing against a granite wall.

"I'm going to put a record on the stereo and dance with you," he said calmly, as though tripping the light fantastic in the Chadwick living room at 3:00 a.m. were the most normal thing in the world. "Although you could persuade me that going to bed would be much more interesting."

"If that's what you have in mind, you should be in Mrs. Cortland's living room, not mine!" Lesley could have bitten off her tongue for putting such a weapon in his hands.

"So you noticed. Do I detect a note of jealousy?"

"You're crazy!"

"Shhh—some people are trying to sleep."

"A good idea. Good night." She turned to leave the room, but was caught and pulled up against his broad chest.

"Good. Might as well skip the dancing—it's just an excuse to get close anyway. I like the 'good night' part best, don't you?"

Before Lesley could reply, warm, firm lips

covered her own and she was lost in his embrace once more. Sure and strong, his arms enclosed her and his hands smoothed across her back, up to her neck, pressing her ever closer to his lean strength. Her fingers sought the waving thickness of his hair and slowly explored the outline of his shoulders under his jacket. A great rushing sound filled her ears and a weakness invaded her limbs. How could she succumb to his charms so quickly? She was as shameless as Eve Cortland, as willing as his other female admirers!

This sobering thought gave Lesley the strength to slip away from his embrace. She was surprised that he released her so gently.

"G-Goodnight, Thane," she said quivering as she turned and fled up the stairs.

She never knew whether he answered or not.

Chapter Four

By some miracle, Lesley managed to avoid Thane for the remainder of the weekend. And by the time they met Monday morning, and he grinned at her with those maddening mocking lights in his dark eyes, she was able to ignore him with studied hauteur.

Knowing that their departure date had been set for sometime that week, Lesley resumed questioning him about their destination. Adamant, he refused to tell her anything more than their date of departure.

The day before they were to leave Lesley marched into his office. She had had enough of being treated like a child with secrets and surprises.

She found him sitting at his desk going over

a report she'd given him concerning a campaign to raise funds for a Galapagos/Antarctic expedition. He looked up when she stalked in without knocking. Without a word from him, Lesley immediately felt apologetic and hated herself for it.

"Excuse me, Thane, I'm sorry to interrupt you, but, well, I *have* to know where we're going. I'll need equipment, clothes . . ."

"That's all taken care of," he said dismissively. He turned back to the papers in front of him.

"I beg your pardon, but how could it be taken care of?" Lesley demanded.

Sighing, he closed the folder. Regarding her as one would an angry child, he said, "Angela Nomura is about your size. She collected everything you'll need. We'll be flying into the mountains, so dress in fairly warm clothes for the plane, take a light jacket, two changes of underwear and your toothbrush—nothing else."

"This is all ridiculous! I have to know where we're going, so I can read . . ."

"That's just what I don't want you to do, Les," he explained. "If you're serious about this, you'll want to learn to adapt yourself to any environment you happen to find, not be full of facts and figures—that is, if you're still determined to become a regular on field studies." One dark eyebrow arched in silent query.

Lesley knew now was her chance to cajole, to demand, to assert herself—or, she thought miserably, to deny her ambitions and tell him to forget the whole thing. Stifling these natural responses, she nodded meekly. "I'll see you at dinner, Thane."

Before she reached the door, he said, "Not tonight, Les, but bright and early in the morning. Be ready at six."

Eyes wide and innocent, she turned and smiled. "No problem, Thane—I certainly don't have much to pack!" With a wave, she was gone.

Lesley was sure that he dismissed her interruption and dove back into the report he was reading. She was wrong. Watching her trim figure glide out the door, Thane asked himself one more time: Why am I taking her on this trip? His answers were far from satisfactory —a favor to Graham; a favor to the Institute; a favor to a friend. He knew only too well that the real reason involved large, hopeful blue eyes and a determined mouth that melted all too delightfully against his.

Uttering a low curse, Thane tried his best to get back to business. It was a tribute to his discipline that he eventually succeeded.

Lesley hummed to herself as she went back to her office. First on her agenda was a meeting between Society members from Texas and Institute researchers currently studying the ecological aftermath of oil spills. She then screened a documentary on beluga whales and orcas, or "killer whales," which Ben Adams and his team had filmed the month before. Finally she penned an official thank-you to the mayor of a small desert community that had assisted a field team studying desert ecology. Not until later, when she had shared a small joke with Mrs. Crandall, did she wonder where Thane might be dining that night. Muttering that it didn't make the slightest bit of difference where Thane Fraser chose to dine, Lesley turned to her typewriter and plunged into another project.

Somehow she managed to ignore the conviction that their dining room would be dishearteningly empty when only she and Graham sat down to one of Harry's marvelous meals. However disturbing it had been at first, Lesley had to acknowledge that Thane's challenging presence added an intensity to her life. Thane made her mad, but he also made her laugh; he'd teased her and he'd kissed her—twice. Lesley couldn't allow herself to examine that too closely. All she could admit was that the life she'd led without him now paled beside the experience of the past week.

"It should be a fascinating trip," she murmured as she rescheduled her appointments for the following week.

True to his word, Thane was waiting outside her bedroom door when she emerged at 6:00 A.M. Stifling a yawn, Lesley mumbled, "Good morning."

She was answered by a knowing grin from

Thane, which quickly turned to a smile of appreciation as he took in her outfit. Lesley had arisen extra early in order to look her best. Her dark shoulder-length hair was brushed smoothly over her shoulders, her makeup was light but carefully applied, and her long-sleeved, slim-fitting apricot wool dress accentuated the soft curves of her figure.

Giving a low whistle, Thane asked, "Are you *sure* you're ready for the wilds?"

Staring steadily at him, Lesley gestured toward the stairs. "Lead the way, Mr. Fraser."

He hesitated only a moment before starting down, carrying one small valise for each of them. As he walked ahead of her, Lesley had the opportunity to study in detail the tan leather jacket and the brown turtleneck that covered wide, straight shoulders. He wore matching tan slacks and soft brown boots, a civilized version of what he would wear in the mysterious mountains that Lesley could not yet name.

In the foyer they were greeted by Graham and Harriet.

"Let me get you something to eat," Harriet begged.

Thane laughed. "There will be breakfast on the plane, Harry." He kissed her cheek. Harriet flushed with pleasure, but she didn't look appeased.

"Bah! Plastic food and little bitty forks," she huffed.

Graham shook his head and hugged his niece. "Come back to me safe and sound, Lesley, dear," he said softly. It was the first time she had left their home since she'd finished college and joined the Institute a year before. Suddenly, she felt homesick and lonely for the man who had meant everything to her during that time.

"Oh, Uncle Graham, don't worry. I'll be fine . . . uh, we both will," she answered, a bit flustered at playing out this sentimental scene under Thane's mocking gaze. But when she stole a look at him, he was smiling gently.

"I'll take good care of her, Graham," he promised. The two men shook hands. With a quick glance at his watch, Thane added, "Ready, Les?"

Just as Thane opened the front door for her, Lesley asked, "Are we meeting the others at the airport?"

Thane hesitated a fraction of a second. He glanced at Graham, who merely shrugged. "No others, Les. Just us."

Without stopping to gauge Lesley's reaction to this news, Thane ushered her out the door and into the taxi he'd called earlier. They both waved as the vehicle pulled away.

Once they were out of sight, Lesley had a great deal to say. "What do you mean, we're going out alone?" she hissed.

"It seems clear to me," he answered, unperturbed.

"How . . . why . . . oh, Thane, we can't go alone," she argued. She was uneasy for reasons that she couldn't even express. She didn't want to reveal *all* her feelings to him.

"It's a week's trip, for no other reason than to get me back in harness and to give you experience, right? It wouldn't be fair to tie up other personnel."

"Surely a field team could find something . . ."

"I didn't say they wouldn't. In fact, we'll be laying the groundwork for a future expedition with a full crew. It won't be the first trip there, but things have changed and could bear further study. Decide now, Les. Have you changed your mind?"

It was obvious—she had two choices: Call off the trip right now or go on his terms. He had trapped her in impossible circumstances. Lesley shook her head stiffly and smoothed her skirt over her knees. Fidgeting with the light coat over her arm, she stared out the window. She would complete this trip in cool silence. Professionalism would be the watchword. If there was ever any chance of friendship and companionship between us, she told herself, he's finally destroyed it.

The silence stretched, tense with her unspoken anger. Finally Thane broke it. "Aren't you going to ask where we're going again?"

Although Lesley was more consumed by curiosity with each passing minute, nothing could induce her to admit it. She stared out the window. Out of the corner of her eye she saw the cab driver shake his head.

"I promised I'd tell you today."

Sighing, Lesley looked at Thane. He grinned back at her confidently. She gripped the worn leather seat and felt a spring about to give way.

"Not going to ask, are you?" His voice hardened. Still Lesley remained silent.

"Idaho," he grated out.

She tilted her head, raised one delicately arched brow. "Mountains?" she asked disinterestedly.

"Sawtooth," he replied, now looking out the window on his side.

"Yes, sir," she said crisply. She went back to her own sight-seeing, even though excitement rendered her incapable of registering the passing scene.

Upon arrival at the airport terminal, Lesley waited with the valises while Thane paid the cabby, who observed rather loudly, "Wives! They're all the same, mister. Guess you ain't been married long?"

Thane smiled at an angry, flushed Lesley. "No, not long at all," he answered. Lesley gasped.

"Well, let me tell you. I think our grandfathers—well, maybe our great-grandfathers—had it right: Keep 'em barefoot 'n pregnant. Either way, mister," he continued, lowering his voice to a whisper. Thane laughed loudly.

Lesley could well imagine what had been said, and she stalked over to give the man a stern piece of her mind. She was forestalled by a firm hand on her arm. "We have a plane to catch, Les," Thane said through his laughter.

Head held high, she stormed into the terminal ahead of him, adamantly holding on to her own valise.

It took her over an hour to calm down. By then they were aloft and heading west.

"Truce, Les?" Thane asked after the stewardess had removed their breakfast trays—Lesley's untouched.

She stared at him mutinously.

"All right. I apologize for not telling you about the trip."

"It's easy to apologize after you have your own way," she whispered.

"I'm far from having my own way with you," he drawled. His gaze rested suggestively on the soft swell of her breasts. Smiling, he patted her hand; when she would have pulled it away, he took hold of it.

"Sorry, Les. I apologize for that, too . . . and for our friendly philosopher behind the wheel. Satisfied?" He sounded sincere, but Lesley was slow to relent.

"I suppose it would make more sense to start off amicably," she finally admitted.

"As head of this expedition, I give that my wholehearted approval."

"All right. I accept your apologies."

Thane shook the hand he was holding. "Like to know more about the trip?"

"As if you didn't know that I'm eaten alive with curiosity!" She laughed. "All I know so far is that this flight is heading to Boise and that we're going into the Sawtooth Mountains."

"You've been a pretty good sport about it, too, Les—and very patient. So you've passed your first test."

"Test!"

"Skill can be learned in time, but nobody can take a course in spirit and patience."

"Couldn't you simply have asked Uncle Graham, or Mrs. Crandall, or even Harry, if I had the necessary qualifications?" she asked, smiling.

"Your own private fan club! Hardly the most objective group."

"*My* fan club? Ever since you arrived, I've thought . . ." Lesley put a hand to her mouth. "I mean, they're just as fond of . . . of you . . . as they are of me, Thane."

He merely nodded, then refused an offer of magazines from the stewardess, who had been particularly attentive to him ever since they'd come aboard. Lesley also refused, without her customary polite smile. Thane didn't seem to notice the woman's interest; Lesley did, and she couldn't say why it irritated her so.

"Anyway," he was saying, "we'll take a chartered flight from Boise to the S and R

Ranch and head into the mountains from there."

"I gather you've been here before?" she asked.

"Often—it's a great place. The *R* stands for Brad Rosemont—my father's cousin and the absentee partner. I spent a lot of time here while I was growing up—even worked as a ranch hand for a couple of summers. The Society has used it as a base before."

"And the *S*?"

"Saunders—Jason and Trevor—they're brothers and have run the place since their father retired. Jason and Phyllis, his wife, live up here with their four kids, and Trevor spends most of his time in his cabin, nearby. Trev's a vet, recently licensed, so he's pretty busy."

"Are there many ranches around?"

"No. Government regulations severely restrict use of these lands—they can't be subdivided—but everyone who lives there likes it that way. You'll like these people— Phyllis is quite a woman. She was a teacher when Jason married her, so now she teaches the older kids at home."

"Are they that isolated?"

"There are three towns, but they're spread out and very, very small. Enough from me. What do you know about the area?"

Lesley nibbled at her lower lip as she searched her mind for information she'd read in reports. Finally she ventured, "Sawtooth

National Recreation Area, Basques, sheep and cattle—lakes, columbine, and . . . and the Salmon River!" she finished triumphantly.

"Are you sure you didn't read my mind?" he teased, obviously pleased with her knowledge.

"Not about our destination," she murmured, lowering her eyes.

"Touché, Les," Thane said, grinning. "But I'm not apologizing. After all, the cab driver said . . ."

"Never mind!" she interrupted, laughing. "I don't think I want to know."

"Probably not," he agreed. "Now, would you like to rest or hear more about the Sawtooths?"

"More, Thane. I want to know as much as I can before we get there."

"Fine, Les. Now you've passed test number two."

She groaned. "When can I just relax and enjoy the ride? I feel as though I were back in school, at exam time."

"Sorry. But there were a few things I had to know. As for the rest of the trip, consider the jury dismissed and the trial over, okay?"

"Wonderful. Now, tell me everything you know about the Sawtooths."

"Everything?"

"Absolutely."

"Then I'd better call the stewardess. We'll have to circle Boise for a few extra hours."

"So knowledgeable?" she teased.

He nodded. It piqued her that he could so unabashedly credit himself with vast knowledge on the area. But when he began talking, Lesley had to admit that he wasn't just boasting. There seemed no end to the facts he tossed off about the mountains, the valleys, the ranch, and the flora and fauna that called them home.

At one point she stopped him. "I'll never remember half of this!" she lamented.

"Just get the flavor of it—specifics can come later."

"Hmmm," she deliberated, "the flavor of it. You spent so much time there, and you're obviously under its spell—so tell me moments, not facts and figures—make me see it." In her intensity she had put a hand on his arm; her face moved in closer to his.

Thane studied the delicate features a moment before he turned to stare silently out the small window. Then, in a low voice, without looking at her, he began to tell her of his feelings for this country. He told her of rock climbing, of a spring so short and a summer so brief as to be almost nonexistent, of lakes strung together like beads on a rosary, of encounters with the various wild animals there. Soon Lesley was lost in the wild mountains and deep valleys he'd learned to treasure.

It was a shock to both of them to find Lesley's hand held securely in Thane's when the intercom announced their arrival in Boise.

Self-consciously removing her hand, Lesley said, a bit breathlessly, "I . . . I think we lost track of time."

"That's what the mountains can do to you. Ready for them?" he asked softly.

Inwardly, she was unsure, even afraid. Outwardly, she smiled and nodded.

After that things moved so fast that Lesley scarcely knew what was happening. Thane hurried her from the large plane to a much smaller craft. Minutes after landing in Boise, they were aloft again, but this time the sensation of flight, and the awesome views left her speechless.

At the end of the brief flight, the plane headed for an airstrip in a valley that looked so tiny between jagged peaks that Lesley closed her eyes and held her breath. Thane chuckled and reached for her hand.

"Relax, Les," he said directly into her ear, for the small plane was noisy. "Bob makes this run all the time."

Still she sat stiffly, heart pounding. She didn't want to tell Thane, but this was her first flight in a small plane. He put his arm around her and pulled her close. Lesley welcomed the embrace, the hard strength against her cheek, the steady beat of his heart in her ear, the clean, fresh smell of his after-shave.

"Looks as though spring is here," he shouted to the pilot, who nodded.

As the plane touched down, there was a bump, then another, causing Lesley to burrow more closely against Thane's comforting body. His head lowered and his lips brushed her temple and hair. "All safe," he said softly.

Slowly, she extricated herself as the plane taxied to a stop near a small barnlike building. "I . . . I'm not usually such a baby about things," she defended herself, smoothing the skirt of her dress.

"I never said you were."

Lesley searched his face for traces of mockery, but she found none. Somehow this kind, understanding Thane was more difficult to deal with.

"Come on. I'm anxious for you to meet the Saunders clan," he said, helping her to unhook her seat belt. She allowed him to catch her around the waist and lift her down from the plane. As she regained steadiness, he said a few words to the pilot, who was leaving to fly right back to the city.

"Where do we go from here?" she asked, looking dubiously at the small pile of gear that had flown here with them. There was no dwelling, no other person anywhere in sight— just some empty corrals. The view was lovely though. If she weren't so tired, she thought, she'd be glad just to stand here and breathe in this invigorating air and gaze at the rocky, snowcapped mountains in the distance. She bent down and picked a long scarlet flower on a spindly stem. "What's this?"

"Indian paintbrush." He smiled as she tested it for scent. "Not quite as dramatic as long-stemmed roses, is it?"

"In this setting?" She laughed incredulously. "Crabgrass would be dramatic here!" A breeze, sharp with the remembrance of winter, blew her hair around her face. She pushed it back.

He laughed too. "But you do like it?"

Lesley merely nodded. Recovering herself, she asked again, "What now? Will someone . . ."

But Thane was already waving toward a winding dirt track that Lesley hadn't noticed before. Looking now, she could just make out a dust cloud coming around a bend.

Thane turned back to her. "It'll be someone from the S and R. They never miss a plane landing."

Lesley swallowed nervously and smoothed her hair. She didn't feel at her best for meeting people, but that couldn't be helped now. Wishing she had the opportunity to replace her lipstick at least, she picked up her purse from where Thane had put it near the other gear.

"You don't need it—you look beautiful," Thane stated simply. He earned a look of shocked surprise. "That's what you were worrying about, wasn't it?" he asked.

Her reply was lost in the noise of the pickup truck as it approached them. It was driven by a grinning, sandy-haired man about Lesley's age. He screeched to a halt and jumped from the truck.

"Thane!" he shouted, pumping the taller man's hand and pounding him on the back.

"How are you, Trev?" Thane asked cordially.

"Great—we all are. I'd ask you the same, but I'm more interested in the birthday gift you've brought me!" He approached Lesley and took her hand. She smiled uncertainly.

Thane's mouth hardened slightly, but he said smoothly, "Les, this is Trevor Saunders. Trev, Lesley Wallis, my . . . my partner."

Chapter Five

Interested and amazed blue eyes gazed down at her as Trevor shook her hand, but Lesley didn't see them. She was looking at Thane. Partner! Not pupil, or burden, or tenderfoot, but partner! Her gratitude showed in her eyes. It was answered by a large, warm smile from Thane, a smile that stopped her heartbeats more effectively than her fear in the plane.

To mask her reaction, she hurriedly said, "I'm so pleased to meet you, Mr. Saunders."

"It's Trevor, Lesley, and don't forget it. I sure won't forget . . ."

"I think Lesley would welcome a chance to freshen up, Trev. Let's get to the house." Just like Uncle Graham, Lesley thought. Thane could phrase orders in the form of gently persuasive requests. And also like Uncle Graham, his "requests" were always obeyed.

The ride to the house was not long, but extremely dusty. Lesley was grateful for Thane's suggestion that she dress warmly in spite of the high temperatures in New York City. There might be flowers and sunshine here, but the temperatures were considerably cool during spring in the high country. And at night, she knew from her reading, they would sleep in down-filled sleeping bags.

Wedged between the two tall men, Lesley was saved from bouncing around the seat, but when the truck bumped into and out of one particularly deep hole, she was tossed hard against Trev. "Umm, wish we could take that one again," he teased, his eyes twinkling down at her.

"That won't be necessary," Thane said firmly. His arm, which had been resting on the seat behind her, now came around her shoulders to pull her close to him, holding her secure from any more jolts. Trevor observed them a moment, then turned back to his driving.

Trying to appear nonchalant, Lesley stared out the front window. Acres of meadows now in vibrant bloom were surmounted by rocky snow-covered crags, seemingly mere feet away, conspirators in that illusion peculiar to mountain country. Here and there were groups of grazing cattle and even an occasional mounted cowboy, the first Lesley had seen outside of films.

Lesley received another pleasant surprise when the ranch came into view. It was neat, modern, and spacious. Several barns and sheds were situated near a long, rambling, low ranch house. "That's the main house," Trevor informed her.

"Where's your place?" Lesley asked.

"Ah-ha!" Trevor exulted. "Already trying to wangle an invitation from me! I knew you were wild for me from the first!"

"I'm sure *we* won't have time to visit you this trip, Trevor," Thane put in, his voice cold and flat.

"Sorry, pal—I didn't know your brand was on the filly." Trevor winked cheerily at a startled Lesley.

"Wrong again, Trev," Thane said, so softly that Lesley doubted the driver heard him. Carefully, he removed his arm from around her. Lesley didn't have time to react, for they'd arrived at the house. Trevor parked near the porch, which surrounded the house on three sides.

He pressed on the horn several times, although he needn't have bothered. Three small children were already tumbling around the corner of the house, eager to inspect the visitors. Two dogs of uncertain ancestry came with them, barking and whining.

The children stopped abruptly when Thane

and Lesley alighted from the truck. The two smallest hung back, but the older one, a sturdy, towheaded youngster who resembled his Uncle Trevor, tilted his head at their visitors.

"Uncle Thane?" he asked.

As an answer, Thane scooped him up and tossed him, giggling, in the air. For a breath-stopping second, he pretended to drop him, then caught him firmly and turned to Lesley, who was petting the frolicking dogs. "Lesley, this is Kyle T. Saunders, age six—no, seven—leader of the pack." Kyle squirmed and shouted in Thane's arms as he was tickled. Thane nodded to the other children, beginning to move closer now as their curiosity overwhelmed their timidity. "And that's Ben and Carrie. Where's your Mom?" he asked them.

"Right behind you, stranger!" a tall, robust woman in shirt and faded jeans shouted from the porch. Lesley turned to see her and received a warm smile that immediately made her feel at home. Her hostess tried to put some order to long brown hair falling out of its bun.

"Good to see you, Phyll," Thane said, putting Kyle down and giving the woman a big hug. "Do I smell apple pies?"

The three children ran off, shouting and calling, "You're It!" to the accompaniment of much barking from the dogs.

"Best nose in the West," Phyllis remarked wryly, winking at Lesley over Thane's shoulder. When he released her, she said, "Welcome to the S and R, Lesley. Thane told us you'd be coming. Let's all go inside—I have to listen for the baby."

With that she led the way into a rough-hewn but comfortable living room. An enormous stone fireplace dominated the room, its graystone hearth covered with a pile of mending and dozens of assorted toys. Inevitable, Lesley thought, with four children. Lesley gratefully sank into a corner of a deep couch. Trevor sat in an armchair nearby, but, to her consternation, Thane dropped down next to her. Again he rested his arm casually but possessively along the couch behind her.

Phyllis was gone a moment, presumably checking on the sleeping baby. When she returned, she cast a knowing eye at the two on the couch, causing Lesley to squirm uncomfortably.

"Something wrong, partner?" Thane asked, mocking lights in his dark eyes.

"Thane," she whispered to him pleadingly, "please!"

He laughed. But he left his arm where it was. "Everything looks the same, Phyll," he said.

"If that's a comment on my failure to redecorate—I've stopped trying!"

"In his tactful way Thane is trying to say that your home is warm and welcoming," Lesley hurried to say, meaning every word.

This busy, cluttered home reminded Lesley of her own happy childhood—especially after living in the quiet and austere home of her uncle.

Pushing a wayward strand of hair out of her eyes, Phyllis smiled her gratitude. The conversation continued a short while, making Lesley feel completely at home. Then Phyllis smiled and said, "Well, enough of the preliminaries. Would anyone like some pie and a cool drink or coffee?"

"Now you're talking, Phyll," Trevor said. "Why don't you ladies leave us alone for a bit while you're getting things ready?"

With Thane's help Lesley struggled up from the deep, soft cushions. "Trev," she commented, "I consider that a very sexist statement, but I'm going anyway."

Both men grinned as she followed Phyllis from the room. The other woman stopped just long enough to pause at the front door and say, "Kyle, don't let Carrie feed Ben any more worms!" Then she ushered Lesley down a hall. They emerged finally into a kitchen, the size of which staggered Lesley, who was used to Harriet's tidy little room in New York. Rows of pots, some so big Lesley could have planted trees in them, gleamed from a black cast-iron rack above the work island. The sink was restaurant size and the stove had six burners and two ovens.

Observing the fifteen-foot-long trestle table,

Lesley exclaimed, "How many people do you feed every day?"

"Don't let the table frighten you. Once or twice a year it's filled for about a week at a time. Otherwise, we just take up this end." Phyllis grinned.

"Oh. I guess just the family takes up quite a bit of room," Lesley said, a wistful note in her voice. An only child herself, she had never known the trials and joys of being one among many.

"You sound the way Thane did before we unofficially adopted him. Only child too?" Phyllis asked kindly.

Lesley nodded.

Cutting the still-steaming pies, Phyllis asked further, her voice deceptively casual, "Thane always says he wants a big family. Do you agree with him?"

"Yes, that would be nice," Lesley said a bit dreamily. Then her head snapped up. "I mean, I don't know about Thane, but I . . . I mean, whether Thane plans a big family or not . . . that is, we aren't . . . er, won't . . . it doesn't . . ."

Phyllis was looking at her strangely as Lesley stammered on, growing more agitated and more flushed by the second. Her torment ended—she thought—when Thane sauntered in, came up behind her, and put his arm around her waist.

"In her tactful way," he began, mimicking

her, "Lesley is trying to say that we've never discussed it."

If she had been able to explain, she would have, but Lesley found herself stymied by Thane's actions. Everything he'd said and done since their arrival had been calculated to keep their true relationship ambiguous in their hosts' eyes. She turned a questioning stare to him. He grinned at her.

"We *haven't* discussed it, have we, Les?"

Since she couldn't deny the truth of his statement, she remained silent.

Phyllis looked pleased. Lesley couldn't imagine why. There wasn't long to wonder in the bustle of serving the drinks and pie, dishing out ice cream or cheese to those who wanted it, and complimenting the baker when they'd tasted the treat.

"Do you like to bake, Lesley?" Phyllis inquired.

"I used to, but Harry does all that now," she answered, taking a sip of iced tea.

Phyllis shot Thane a sharp look. "Harry?"

"Harriet Brown—Graham and Lesley's housekeeper," Thane told her. Whatever game he was playing with them all, he was enjoying it. Lesley frowned at him.

"Housekeeper!" Trevor shouted. "No wonder you won't look twice at a struggling young vet," he lamented.

Lesley was grateful when the sudden wailing of a baby ended the conversation.

"Duty calls," sighed Phyllis.

Lesley stood up. "Would I frighten her—or him—if I went in?" she asked shyly.

Phyllis sat down again. "Clint is just three months old and not too sure about faces yet. Be my guest, please. But are you sure?"

"I haven't been around a baby since I was about thirteen, but I'd like to try, if you'll trust me."

"Lesley, I'd trust Count Dracula if it would mean five extra minutes of rest!" Everyone laughed. Lesley made her way down the hall, finding the door easily by following the cries of the baby.

The sunny room she entered had seen many babies, as evidenced by the casual clutter of toys and baby clothes. After soothing the fussing infant, Lesley found a fresh diaper, powder, and the diaper pail. She was awkward, but Clint didn't seem to mind. Wrapping him in a light blanket, Lesley cuddled him close, inhaling the irresistible natural perfume of a new baby.

Delighted by the baby's cooing, Lesley walked slowly back to the kitchen. She didn't notice the silence until she finally looked up to find three pairs of interested, amused eyes on her.

"Uh . . . oh . . . I think he's hungry, Phyllis," she said hurriedly, brushing a light kiss on the top of the infant's head and handing him to his mother.

"One thing you have to learn about children, Lesley," Phyllis informed her with a smile, "is that they're born hungry, and they stay that way." She nodded toward the two men, who were busy serving themselves second pieces of pie.

Watching the mother and child, Lesley felt a betraying moistness invade her eyes. She was thankful when Thane took her hand and pulled her down beside him. "Now I know how you stay a bag of bones," he teased. "You haven't finished your pie."

"Some bag of bones!" Trevor commented. "Come rattle around my hut anytime."

"Trevor, you are impossible," Phyllis scolded.

They sat around the table talking until Jason Saunders walked in the back door. He was tall and broad, with deep lines in his face from years of wind and harsh mountain weather.

He was friendly to Lesley, but something more to Thane.

"It's been too long, Thane," Jason said, grasping the younger man's hand and arm with both his huge, work-hardened hands.

Now cuddling a sleeping baby, Phyllis broke in with, "Why don't you men go into the living room? I'll bring you in pie and coffee, honey."

As if just noticing her, Jason turned to his wife, brushed a kiss absentmindedly on her cheek, and patted the baby. "That'd be good, Phyll."

When the low rumble of their voices disappeared down the hall, Phyllis offered to show Lesley her room.

"A shower and a rest would be terrific right about now, Phyllis. Thank you," Lesley said.

Leading the way back to the main entrance, where Lesley collected her purse and valise, Phyllis led her down another hallway and into a small bright room that shared a bath with a connecting room. "Thane will be in there. I hope you don't mind sharing a bathroom?" Phyllis asked, obviously unsure about their relationship.

"We share one at Uncle Graham's. He's used to hunting through cleansing creams to find his after-shave by now, I guess," Lesley assured her hostess.

"Just like being mar . . . I mean, that's good. It won't be a problem then. See you later, Lesley," she called as she left, shutting the door behind her.

Lifting her long, heavy hair off her neck and letting it drop again, Lesley bent to her suitcase. She unpacked the light robe she'd brought and headed for the bathroom. Carefully she locked the door to Thane's room before undressing and pinning her hair up. She couldn't remember a time when a long, hot shower had been more welcome.

Two hours later, Lesley lay sound asleep on her bed, deaf to the sound of a knock on her door. Finally, it opened slightly and Thane looked inside the room. Seeing her asleep, he walked in and stood by her bed for long moments. Her dark hair fanned out around her face, which looked like that of a small girl in her unguarded sleep. Her softly rounded cheeks were still flushed from her shower and her lips were slightly parted.

He leaned close, touched her shoulder. "Les . . . Les, time to wake up."

She stirred, tried to turn over, mumbled something.

"Les!" he said a bit more loudly. Her eyes flew open, stared straight up into his. For seconds she was disoriented, then came fully awake.

He touched her cheek. "Hi, sleepyhead."

"Thane," she murmured, her voice sleep-husky. "What time is it?" She looked around for a clock, trying not to feel self-conscious.

"Does it really make so much difference?" he asked softly, coming closer until he was sitting on the bed beside her.

"Everyone will be expecting us," she answered breathlessly, trying to sit up. A hand on her shoulder prevented her.

"Thane?" Then all words stopped as his mouth came on hers, soft and gentle as the unbidden feelings in her heart for this strong man.

"Mmmm, you smell like lilacs," he sighed against her mouth before taking it again, this time with more demand as he parted her lips. She answered his caress with a depth of feeling that surprised them both. Then he smiled, lowering himself beside her. She could feel his hard sinewy strength and the warmth of him through the thin material of her robe.

Somehow her robe was untied, and his sure, gentle hands were moving over her, exploring her soft curves with tantalizing yet soothing movements. What small protest she might have made was smothered by his lips.

As his fingers trailed over the peak of one rounded breast, she arched against him. "Easy, Les, take your time. This has been brewing since we met. There's no hurry."

His words washed over her like icy water. With a muffled cry, she pushed away from him. He tried to bring her back into his arms, but she was already sitting up on the opposite side of the bed and tying her robe securely around her.

"It must be near dinnertime. Please excuse me, Thane." Her voice was low but cool and firm, belying the turmoil she felt inside.

"Excuse you! What kind of game are you playing, Les? One minute all soft and melting, the next . . ." He rose, too, and walked toward her.

"What are you doing in my room anyway?" she demanded.

He stopped and stood with his hands on his hips. "At the moment, I'm wasting my time talking to you when there are better things we could be doing."

He watched a betraying blush sweep her cheeks. "I came in here in the first place because you locked my door to the bathroom."

"Oh, I'm sorry. I remember now."

He came toward her again. Lesley backed away, an uncertain look on her face.

"And just for the record," he said, "I knocked."

"Thane, I'm . . ."

"Dinner is at six thirty." He gestured to the door he was holding. "Should I lock this behind me or will I be allowed to shower in safety?"

With a frustrated scream, Lesley wrenched the door from his grasp and, ignoring his amused chuckle, slammed it as hard as she could.

After dinner, Lesley watched Thane play with the children. They refused to go to bed until he had told them a story. Finally, off they went, Kyle first, then Ben and Carrie. Thane tucked the two smallest ones under each arm, and they all marched off singing.

"Whew," Phyllis sighed. "Peace and quiet at last! I think I've died and gone to heaven!"

"Now, hon," Jason reminded her, "you always said you wanted ten kids."

"That's when I thought I'd have five and you'd have five!" Everyone laughed. Phyllis added, "It doesn't work that way, Lesley, so be warned!"

"Thanks, Phyllis, I'll remember that." Lesley smiled, feeling herself relax now that Thane's disturbing presence had been removed. She refused another cup of coffee from Trevor, who then invited her to take a walk outside.

"You've never seen stars until you've seen our stars," he informed her.

"*Your* stars—hmmm, now I can't pass up a chance like that. Lead the way." She knew Trevor offered uncomplicated friendliness, and Lesley felt that was just what she needed. Besides, anything was better than sitting here waiting for Thane.

"To think I doubted you," Lesley apologized, marveling at the display in the night sky when they emerged from the porch and walked away from the lights of the house.

"We like it," Trevor said simply, leading her through a gate and into a meadow. Not far away she could hear owls hooting. The air was incredibly clean and crisp.

"No wonder Thane loves this country," Lesley sighed.

"Who?" Trevor asked.

She stopped and looked at Trevor, a dark shadow near her. "Thane." Realizing his meaning, she hastened to add, "I'm sorry, Trev. It's just that Tha . . . I mean, he's the head of our little expedition, you know, and . . ."

"Give me credit for knowing a bit more than

I seem to, Lesley," Trevor interrupted. "Come on. Let's walk a little farther."

Unable to explain her feelings for Thane, she obeyed.

They had gone only a few steps when Lesley slid on a small rock in her path, twisting her ankle. Immediately Trevor was kneeling beside her while she rested a hand on his shoulder. He examined the ankle with gentle fingers, pronounced it just slightly bruised, and stood up.

"I'm sorry to be so clumsy," Lesley said, then: "Trevor! What are you doing?"

He was picking her up to carry her back to the house. "Really," she laughed, "if you'll just give me a strong shoulder to lean on, I can walk on my own."

"Now what trouble could it be to heft a little bag of bones like you?" he teased. Effortlessly, he strode off. They were still laughing and arguing the point when a harsh voice interrupted them. "Excuse me if I'm interrupting anything, but just what is going on out here?"

"Lesley twisted her ankle, Thane, and . . ."

"Never mind telling me all the details. Let's just get her back to the house as quickly as possible," Thane cut in harshly.

Inside, Trevor lowered Lesley gently down on a chair. He removed her shoe and moved her foot carefully. The sharp pain caused her to flinch. "Just as I thought," he said. "A simple bruise. You'll be fine in the morning."

"Are you sure?" Thane asked impatiently.

"I'm sure," Lesley said firmly. "We'll leave as planned." She met Thane's cold gaze without wavering.

"Be ready at five thirty, promptly," Thane said. "You're old enough to know what you're doing."

Chapter Six

Leslie dressed hastily and tiptoed to the kitchen, where she found Phyllis humming and busy. The baby was contentedly napping in a cradle in the corner. The electric lights were on, for it was barely light outside.

"I guess he's had his breakfast already?" Lesley asked, peeking at the sleeping infant.

"Yes, Clint dines before dawn. He's good for two hours or so now—long enough to get some laundry done and feed the others."

"You work hard," Lesley observed.

Phyllis stopped breaking eggs into a bowl. "Funny, I never think about it much. Don't you repeat this to any of those men, but I love every minute of it."

"You mean you love Jason and those children," Lesley interpreted softly.

For just a second a becoming softness stole over the strong, capable features as she nodded, but it was immediately replaced by the businesslike expression Phyllis usually wore. Then she resumed her work with an efficiency that left Lesley gasping.

At one point in the headlong pace of their breakfast preparations Phyllis asked, "How's your ankle, Lesley?"

"I'd almost forgotten about it," she lied. "Thane just fusses too much."

Jason and Trevor came through the back door, greeting the women. Within moments the three children were also at their places, and the task of serving a meal to this large group began.

The door burst open and Thane strode in, shouting, "Lesley! Phyll, have you seen . . ." His look fell on a smiling Lesley, seated next to Trevor. Running agitated fingers through his hair, he strode out again.

Phyllis laughed. "Your brother doesn't seem to be in the best of moods this morning," she remarked. "What did you do to upset him?"

Trevor shrugged. "I can't imagine. Maybe he has problems. Maybe Della's giving him grief—"

"Who's Della?" Lesley asked before she could stop herself.

Phyllis looked apprehensively at Trevor. "Thane's cousin," she replied. "She was here a few years ago . . ." Phyllis's eyes shifted and she suddenly became absorbed in dividing the piece of toast between Ben and Carrie.

"She was here all right!" Jason laughed. "She's some girl. We even thought that she and Thane were—" As if a thought had suddenly struck him, he stared at Lesley, then at his wife's exasperated expression.

Lesley kept her eyes on her plate. She wished she could disappear into the floor.

"I didn't mean anything by it, Lesley," Jason blundered on. "That is, she's an old friend, and when I asked Thane about her, he said he'd seen her the night before you left New York, and . . . I mean . . . he . . . they . . . she . . ." Helplessly, he looked for aid from Trevor, who merely raised his eyebrows and shook his head.

Lesley stood, pushing her chair out so quickly that it nearly fell over. "Please excuse me, everyone. I'm sure Thane is ready to leave now. Thank you all, for everything."

Jason was in her path. "I'm sorry, Lesley. I've got a big mouth."

Lesley smiled at him. "Don't worry about it, Jason. Thane and I are . . . merely partners."

Head high, she went out to Thane, who was waiting for her on the front porch.

He was talking to two ranch hands, whom he introduced to Lesley as Curly and Sig. They tipped their hats and sauntered off toward the barns. Lesley patted the nose of one of the horses whose reins Thane held. A brown mare with a blaze of white down her face, she stood placidly waiting to begin work.

"Are we ready?" Lesley asked brightly.

"Don't you mean, are *you* ready? I got the impression you'd prefer to stay here in Trev's very willing company." He tossed a stirrup over the saddle and checked the cinch on his mount—a gray gelding that shifted nervously.

Lesley's temper flared. "And you'd rather be back in New York—in Della's company."

He grinned maddeningly. "Jason's been talking out of turn?"

She turned a cool face to him. "Not at all. I couldn't care less what you do."

"I could make you retract that," he warned. Lightly he slapped his horse's rump and moved closer to Lesley.

"Please don't," she said.

Grasping the saddle horn with both hands, Thane mounted his horse with one lithe jump and slipped his booted feet in the stirrups. "Let's go."

As they rode off toward the mountains, the Saunders clan came out onto their front porch to wave them off. Watching the two riders until they were around the outbuildings, Kyle turned to his father. "Why was Uncle Thane so cross?"

Glancing at a smiling Trevor, Jason shrugged, still uncomfortable after his *faux pas* earlier. "That, son," he drawled, ruffling the boy's already unruly curls, "is a question

I'll let your mother answer—in about ten years."

Lesley had had enough. For two hours they had not exchanged a word. Deciding that their behavior was more appropriate for Kyle and Carrie than for adults, she said lightly, "I've heard of silent mountain vastnesses, but I never thought I'd find myself in vast mountain silences."

He was still quiet for so long that she thought her feeble attempt had failed completely.

"I hope you never have to make your living writing jokes," he said, his back to her as he rode ahead of her up a steep slope. The landscape had steadily gotten rockier and more rugged as they'd moved into the heavier forests.

"Maybe I was desperate for some companionship," she retorted.

"Don't you like Bunny?"

"Who's Bunny?"

He turned to her. "Not who—what. You're sitting on her." He smiled, making everything all right again.

Lesley made a face. "If you say so. But isn't that a . . ."

Thane laughed. " . . . a terrible name. But don't tell Carrie—she chose it when the mare was broken to the saddle last year."

"In that case, girl," Lesley said, patting the glossy neck, "Bunny you are."

From that initial awkwardness things progressed pleasantly between Lesley and her companion. The release of tension left Lesley free to marvel at the magnificence all around her. Now and then they would sight a mountain bluebird, which, Thane informed her, was Idaho's state bird. Other birds, mostly unseen, gave the lie to tales of quiet woods.

Once Lesley discovered an elk making its way to a stream. She pointed it out to Thane.

"Think you're something, don't you?" he teased, following the direction of her pointing finger.

She grinned at him, allowing her red cowboy hat to slide to rest on her back, held by its tie at her neck.

"What would you do if I told you there was a bear rooting around a boulder just a few yards off the trail we're on?" he asked mildly.

Swallowing bravely, Lesley gripped the saddle horn. She looked nervously around her. "I'd do whatever you told me to do," she whispered. "Where is it?"

He laughed loudly. "No bear, Les," he managed to say.

"Why, you . . ."

"I just asked what you would do if I told you."

They rode in peaceful silence into a valley with a lake set in it like a jewel. In spite of the distractions of the countryside Lesley was feeling the protest of muscles used to an infrequent horseback ride in the park, not this sustained effort over rough terrain. She began to shift her weight uncomfortably in her saddle.

"We're almost there," he remarked. "I planned a short ride for today."

"That was considerate," Lesley allowed. "Not that I am at all tired, of course—"

"Of course. Well," he said, "think of the horses at least."

"I'd forgotten," she murmured, leaning forward to rub Bunny's neck.

"Our campsite is just up here." He pointed to a rocky outcropping close above the jewel-like lake in the shelter of some trees. "Approve?"

"You don't need to ask. I feel like Snow White discovering a magic glade."

"Well, you look like one of the dwarfs— Sleepy, to be exact. Let's set up camp, make some lunch, and see to the horses. Then we'll do some exploring after you rest."

True to his word, Thane tended the horses, set up camp, and served a cold lunch—with a little help from his partner. Then he insisted she lie down for an hour.

"I'm too excited to sleep," Lesley pleaded, refusing to lie down on the sleeping bag he'd unpacked.

"Either you get some rest or no surprise this afternoon."

"Tyrant! Anyone would think I was about three years old."

"If the shoe fits . . ." he drawled, settling

himself on the other sleeping bag, near hers. Pulling his hat over his eyes, he gave every appearance of drifting off to sleep. Lesley sighed and flopped down, grumbling. In minutes she was breathing regularly in a gentle sleep.

"Hunting? For what?" Lesley panted.

Thane stopped climbing, turned to her. "Unicorns. What else?"

Lesley noticed he wasn't even breathing hard. She grimaced at his back and plunged doggedly on—up, always up. Lesley sighed. She kept herself in good condition, she thought, by walking and biking in the park, but it hadn't prepared her for the Sawtooths. Every muscle cried out in protest at the strain of rock-climbing after their ride. Her lungs ached from the effort to breathe at this altitude. She was just about to swallow her pride and ask to rest when Thane stopped on a ledge close to the dizzying plunge of a silvery waterfall.

With a moan, Lesley collapsed against the rock wall. She closed her eyes and didn't open them until Thane nudged her shoulder and put a pair of binoculars in her hands.

"Let's get to work," he ordered, lying on his stomach beside her, his elbows braced on the very edge of the precipice. Lesley took a deep breath and joined him, but a few inches back from the edge.

Scanning the peaks around them with his

binoculars, Thane murmured, "You take the area to the right. I'll take the left."

Obediently, Lesley started her search. After a moment, she stopped and turned to him. "Tell me again what I'm looking for?"

"I told you, uni . . ."

"Thane!"

"Quiet," he reprimanded her. "You'll frighten them away."

"I think all this clean mountain air has gotten to you," she whispered.

"Perhaps, but today I feel lucky. I've tried to see one here before, but never managed. You'll bring me luck."

Intrigued but curious, Lesley asked, "I must be as crazy as you, but I'll bite—how could I possibly make a difference?"

"Know the unicorn legend?"

"Dozens of them. Which do you want?" Lesley smiled, for she had made a hobby researching the unicorn myths, prompted by Graham's whimsical naming of his organization.

"Then you know that unicorns will always come to fair maidens."

Lesley laughed. This discussion was getting her nowhere. She decided to make the best of it and enjoy the breathtaking scenery.

They lay in silence for nearly an hour. Twice Lesley sighted an eagle gliding on air currents above them, and she was able to use her binoculars on a black bear with two cubs, rooting around in some rocks far below them.

Once she was sure she had seen a mountain lion, though Thane told her it was just a shadow.

Finally a sharp movement from Thane gained Lesley's attention. Pointing to an almost sheer rock wall to their left, perhaps a hundred yards away, he motioned her to keep silent. Lesley peered through the glasses.

There, poised majestically where there looked to be no foothold, was a magnificent bighorn ram.

Lesley stared while Thane managed to take several pictures of it before some slight movement or sound sent the alert beast racing up the cliff and out of sight.

"I never dreamed . . ." she breathed, sitting up and pushing loose strands of hair back from her face.

To her surprise, Thane leaned over and kissed her cheek. "You brought me luck, just as I thought you would, Les," he said. His face came close. His fingers touched her hair.

Flushing, Lesley scrambled up and dusted off her jeans. "It'll be dark soon. Shouldn't we get some more exploring done before we call it a day?"

Thane remained seated on the ledge. "In a minute. After one question."

"All right, but just one," she said.

"You know, Les, everybody in the world has a dream." She nodded, puzzled. He went on, "For Graham, dreams are embodied in the symbol of the unicorn. After knowing you this past week or so, I wonder: What's your unicorn, Lesley Wallis? What kind of dream are you working for at the Institute or here, on a mountain with someone you hardly know?"

From somewhere she found a light tone. "No fair. You said one question."

He stared at her, his features serious.

Lesley looked at her hands. It was becoming alarmingly, heartbreaking clear to her that whatever her answer might be, if she were truthful, her dream would have to include the tall man at her side.

Someone I hardly know? she asked herself. I feel I know Thane better than I've known anyone in my life.

"Is that such a hard question, Les?" he asked quietly.

"Not hard, exactly, just . . . unexpected," she stalled. After thinking a few moments, she said, "My own particular 'unicorn' is much like Uncle Graham's—a world of peace and knowledge, a good world for humans and other animals."

"Nothing for yourself?"

Lesley looked at him, then looked away to stare off at the endless vistas stretching from horizon to horizon. Gesturing expansively, she said, "With all this at my feet, wouldn't I be selfish to ask for more?" She smiled, but the smile became more and more uncertain as Thane rose and came to stand beside her. Lesley felt he was as strong and compelling as these mountains—and just as unreachable.

He put out his hand. "Leave it for now, Les. But I'm beginning to see why you're such a success in public relations work."

Taking her hand, he led her down to their camp. They slid down loosely rocked slopes and stumbled over exposed roots of trees.

Lesley tried not to think what the rest of the evening would bring. If she weren't on her guard, she knew, she would be in danger of falling—not down the mountain, but into dangerous love with this "someone she hardly knew."

Chapter Seven

With tips from Thane, Lesley amazed herself with the quality of the meal she was able to prepare. They were "roughing it," just as he'd promised, but modern methods of freeze-drying foods meant that supplies could be packed for long distances and transformed into near-gourmet meals even over a tiny camp stove.

Thane and Leslie were relaxing by the campfire after a leisurely dinner when Thane remarked calmly, "You're welcome to zip your sleeping bag with mine tonight."

"I thought I made it clear..." Lesley began.

Thane laughed. "It's just that it gets very cold up here soon, and body heat is unbeatable."

"Is that how you kept Della warm?" These ill-considered words were spoken before Lesley really had a chance to think. Horrified, she put a hand over her mouth.

"I don't believe you really want an answer to that," he said.

"Thane, I'm . . ." she faltered.

"Forget it, Les. Good night." With that, he put out the small fire in the stove, picked up his sleeping bag, and moved to the other side of their campsite, leaving her more alone than she'd ever felt in her life.

It was late when she finally dozed off; still, she found no real rest. The ground was hard. And he was right, she thought ruefully. It was very cold. She tucked her head inside the bag; nevertheless, she tossed and turned, half dozing and seeking to contort into the slight warm spot she made. It was some time before she finally dropped off to sleep.

Mmmm, she thought, being snug in bed has to be one of the pleasantest sensations around. She snuggled closer to her source of warmth, then her eyes flew open. Warm! How? Moving her hand, she encountered the firm, solid feel of a man's wool-covered chest.

With a scream of outrage, Lesley tried to leap up. Laughing, Thane held her down, pinning her flailing arms above her head.

"I wondered when you'd wake up." He grinned, looming uncomfortably close above her.

"You despicable, unprincipled, cheating . . . " she screamed at him.

He clucked his tongue at her and shook his head. "Is that any way to talk to your rescuer?"

"I don't know what you're talking about. Let me go!" She squirmed against him, to no avail. One long, sinewy leg captured both of hers under it.

"Your tossing and turning and grumbling were keeping me awake, so I moved in with you. I told you body heat was your best bet— you slept like an angel."

His gaze dropped down to where her light shirt had come unbuttoned, probably from all her exertions during the night. She had removed the bulky wool shirt for sleeping, but now how she wished she'd left it on! Her breasts were almost totally exposed to his gaze. In spite of the chill of the early morning, Leslie felt a betraying warmth steal up from her toes. Her breathing practically stopped.

Slowly, slowly, his eyes examined the bounty displayed so unwillingly before him. Leslie made little frustrated sounds deep in her throat. He forced her gaze back up to her face, over her lips, and to her imploring eyes.

She tried to talk, to reintroduce sane reason into this tense situation, but his lips silenced her. Once, twice, featherlight kisses teased her mouth, pressed upon her cheeks, her forehead, her jaw, back to her mouth, finally to her eyes, which closed in surrender to his touch.

His arms released her arms, which then slid inside his shirt almost of their own volition to caress the muscled chest against which she so recently had lain in peaceful slumber.

"Les, Les," he murmured softly as his head lowered over one perfect round breast, exciting it to taut urgency with his lips.

He slipped her shirt off her shoulders and shrugged out of his own. When she shivered, he covered her body with his, eliciting a soaring response from her at the hard contact of his skin. Long moments passed in meltingly sweet kisses, drugging caresses. In spite of her arousal, Leslie tried to push him away.

Suddenly, out of the immense silence that surrounded them, three small explosions in quick succession rent the quiet.

Thane lifted his head abruptly with an ease that cut Lesley to the quick. She herself was incapable of movement, drowning as she was in desire and now, to her dismay, in frustration.

Muttering a curse, Thane leaped out of their snug bed, pulling his clothes on before Lesley managed to say, "Thane, what is it? What's . . ."

"Get dressed, Les. We're about to have company." He ran his fingers through his hair, pulled on his heavy outer shirt against the early-morning chill, and sat down to jerk on his socks and boots, all with vicious, angry movements.

Pushing her tousled hair out of her eyes, Lesley blinked disbelievingly. "How—who could be here now?" she mumbled, shivering.

Thane kneeled beside her. He shook her slightly. "Les! Get dressed. Those three shots, in case you were not aware, are a signal in these parts that a camp is about to have unexpected company. Now I'll go meet whoever it is and stall them, but hurry!"

Shakily, she searched for her shirt, buried in the tumbled folds of the two bags zipped together as one. Holding the shirt over her breasts, she insisted, "I'm not getting up until you're gone."

"Fine time to be modest," he growled, getting up and turning his back to her. "I'll be back in about three minutes. So *move!*" He stalked out of the campsite.

Scrambling around to find her clothing, Lesley finally managed to dress, comb her tangled hair, and achieve some semblance of calm. Just as she heard voices entering the grove, she ran to the sleeping bags, unzipped them, and tossed Thane's aside in a heap. If only I could push away my feelings as easily! she thought.

She turned a smooth, calm countenance to their early-morning visitor. To her chagrin, it was Trevor Saunders who walked into camp, leading his horse. He and Thane were frowning and talking earnestly in low tones.

Stepping toward them, Lesley said brightly, "Morning, Trev." If her voice sounded a bit forced, at least she knew that only Thane would guess at the reason why.

"Les . . ." Thane began, almost hesitantly.

Ignoring Thane, Lesley continued, "We were . . . uh . . . lazy this morning, but I'll have breakfast ready in no time." She didn't notice that the two men were staring at her. "Thane, please light the stove," she added, hoping to break the awkward silence.

Instead Thane put his hands on her shoulders and held her. "Les, Trev came up here because something's happened."

"Some—something's happened? Tell me, Thane—what is it?" Thane held her close to his lean warmth. Trevor turned away, ostensibly to loosen the cinch on his saddle.

Thane stroked her hair. "It's Graham, Les. He's in the hospital. A heart attack."

Lesley pushed away and stared at the face that had been close to hers just moments before but in quite a different context. "Is he . . . has he . . . ?"

"He's all right, and Dr. Bailey is hopeful."

Breaking away, Leslie looked wildly about the camp. "I must get to him, right away. To the ranch, Trev—take me there, and I can get . . ."

"Les!" Thane urged. "The first thing to do is calm down—you're not doing anybody any good by panicking. Now we'll have some breakfast, because we all need it, and then we'll all go back. You'll be with Graham by this evening, I promise."

Chapter Eight

"Are you sure, Dr. Bailey?" Lesley pleaded.

Dr. Bailey smiled down into red-rimmed eyes dulled with lack of sleep. These last three days nothing would persuade her to leave the hospital.

"He's doing better than a man half his age could expect to do, Miss Wallis. In fact, he's probably doing better than you at the moment. Please, at the risk of sounding inhospitable. . . ." He paused to let his pun sink in, but Lesley didn't react. "Go home, my dear young lady. You didn't look well when you got here and now you look even worse. Anyway, anyone who can't find the energy to at least groan at one of my puns is in a bad way."

To appease him, Lesley smiled, but it faded

as quickly as it had appeared on her pale, drawn features.

"I'm afraid to leave him, doctor. I was only gone twenty-four hours, and look what happened . . ." She stopped and wiped at a tear trying to fall.

Dr. Bailey smiled. "Rest assured, Miss Walis, the sudden absence of a lovely woman, tragic as that may well be, does not precipitate coronaries." As if something had suddenly occurred to him, he amended, "At least not in men like Graham Chadwick."

"I suppose I'm being silly."

"Just a mite overprotective. Now, will you take my advice?"

"She certainly will, doctor," said a soft but commanding voice a few feet away from them in the wide, tiled hallway.

Turning in surprise, Lesley found herself staring directly into familiar dark eyes set in the delicate face of a woman about Graham's age. Softly curling gray hair framed an unlined, still beautiful face. Smiling gently, the woman held out a slim, long-fingered hand, and said, "I'm Lydia Fraser, Lesley. I've been anxious to meet you."

"How . . . how could you know . . ." Lesley asked. Then she figured out the answer. "Thane," she said flatly. Just thinking about him gave her pain. She had neither seen nor talked to him since their nightmare trip from Idaho. It was agonizing to know that he was

satisfied with the current state of affairs—
that the intimacy horribly interrupted by Trev
had only been a passing whim, an instant of
desire. True, he had communicated with Graham by phone, had sent flowers to him, but he
had made no effort to get in touch with Lesley
after their rather hurried farewells.

"Naturally, dear," the woman said in a
quiet voice. "And now that I'm here, you must
go home and let that amazing woman—Mary?
—care for you."

"Harry—really Harriet," Lesley laughed.
"But I don't think . . ."

"You've been doing entirely too much thinking. I plan to stay until you're able to come
back in, say, twenty-four hours or so. And
that's that," she added with finality when
Lesley opened her mouth to protest.

Just then the elevator door beside them
opened and Thane stepped out. Without a
word, he walked up to Lesley and studied her
face with the same disturbing intensity employed by his mother moments before.

"You look terrible," he said without preamble.

Before Lesley could answer him, his mother
put in smoothly, "Really, Thane, the poor girl
has been through a lot."

"You have no idea," he muttered.

Knowing only too well to what he referred,
Lesley turned away, staring at her hands.

"How is Graham doing?" Thane asked.

"Much better, dear. I heard the doctor telling Lesley so." At Lesley's startled glance, Lydia colored. "I'm not in the habit of eavesdropping, Lesley, but I didn't want to interrupt."

"That's all right, Mrs.—uh, Lydia." She looked at the soft blue leather tote Thane carried. It was brimming with various colors of yarn, needles, and several books and magazines.

"Your bag, Mother," Thane said, handing it to Lydia. Leslie found it difficult to take her eyes from Thane's lean form, dressed in gray slacks and a light gray shirt and jacket.

"Thank you, dear," Lydia said. "As you can see, Lesley, I'm prepared for a long siege. Perhaps," she added wistfully, "finding me here will be a nice surprise for Graham." She looked almost doubtful.

Kissing her cheek, Thane said, "You know very well you'll be the best medicine he's had. I'll call you later." Lydia smiled and walked toward the glassed-in waiting room, for it wasn't yet visiting hours in the cardiac care unit. She called a cheery "Good-bye for now" to Lesley.

"If you'll excuse me, Thane," Lesley said coldly, "I'll go and keep your mother company."

Before she could go two steps, Thane had pinned her elbow in a hard grasp. "You're going home—with me." His fingers bit into her tender skin.

"That'll be the day," Lesley hissed. "Now let go of me or I'll make a scene."

"Then you'll get us both thrown out. This is a cardiac unit, remember. If you have no consideration for yourself, have some for other people."

"Me!" she nearly shouted, outraged.

But he wasn't listening. He'd already summoned the elevator. As though she were a recalcitrant child, he shoved her into it. Lesley stood there staring at the numbered buttons as if they were some important message to decipher. In spite of herself she was shaking, unable to combat his highhanded actions. She chanced a look at his hard, tanned jaw, where a muscle was jerking in anger. Once more she abandoned herself to his dictates.

"What *have* you been *doing* to yourself, Miss Lesley? It's a wonder Mr. Graham didn't have a relapse just seeing you like this!" Harriet fussed, relieving Lesley of purse and jacket. She practically pushed her into a living room chair.

"I told her the same thing, Harry," Thane agreed. There were mocking lights in his dark eyes, so like his mother's. Aware of her perverse joy simply at seeing him again, Lesley turned away.

"You did not!" she protested. "You just said . . ."

"Never mind that now, Les," he interrupted her smoothly. "Just do as Harry says."

Powerless, she found herself herded into her room and then plunked into a steaming bubble bath scented with her favorite lily-of-the-valley fragrance. There she soaked away the tensions of the past days—at least until a knock sounded at the door and Thane said, "Are you coming down to dinner or should I come in there and fish you out?"

Lesley sat up quickly, sloshing water and trails of bubbles over the side of the tub onto the yellow tiled floor. "I'm coming, I'm coming," she answered hastily.

She brushed her hair out, tied it back with a green ribbon, and slipped into her favorite robe—the one Uncle Graham had given her two Christmases ago. Deciding to remain barefooted, she stepped out into the hall. She found Thane waiting for her. Arms folded, he lounged patiently against the door frame. He had also changed into more casual clothes—denims and a brown shirt that accentuated his tan and his penetrating dark eyes.

"That's better," he said, admiring her changed appearance.

"So glad you approve," Lesley replied sarcastically as she brushed by him.

"Oh, I do, most definitely. Like proof?" he asked, reaching for her hand.

She slipped away from him and ran down the stairs. "In a word, no," she tossed back over her shoulder. Why should she consent to have her heart broken?

* * *

For Harriet's benefit Thane and Lesley made polite conversation at dinner, concentrating on Society projects, especially the sea mammal documentary Lesley had screened before their trip and Graham's attack. Lesley was sure they'd hidden their antagonism until Harry snorted, "Anybody'd think there was two enemies sittin' here. I think I'll just go to bed and leave you two to fight it out."

"Nobody puts one over on Harry," Thane commented.

Lesley took a last forkful of her cheesecake, dabbed at her mouth with her napkin, and rose. "I think I'll get a book and go upstairs."

He stood up. "I'd like to talk to you first."

Knowing protest was useless, Lesley led the way into the den where Graham kept most of his books and busied herself choosing a mystery from her uncle's vast collection. Thane sat down on the couch and leaned back and stretched like some supremely contented jungle cat.

Holding her book like a shield over her fast-beating heart, Lesley walked past him to the door. "First I'm going to call the hospital."

"No need. I called while you were getting ready for dinner. Graham was too busy to talk."

"Busy? Is everything all right?" Lesley exclaimed.

"He was busy talking to my mother. It takes

a little while to catch up on the thirty-three years since they've seen each other."

She regarded him in puzzlement. "How do you know it's been exactly thirty-three years?" she asked, curious in spite of herself. She and her mother knew little of Graham's past because they hadn't lived right in New York City and Graham had traveled so much.

"My age plus, oh, about one and a half years."

"That's very interesting, but what has your age got to do with it?" she pursued, even more curious.

"You didn't know that Graham almost married my mother?"

She shook her head.

"Unlike her son, the gypsy, Mother is a homebody. Graham's work, his traveling, the danger he was in so often—she couldn't face it. Along came my father—a quiet, settled soul," Thane told her, his voice becoming low and far away when he spoke of his late father. He stared at his hands. Abruptly he shook off the mood. "Anyway, they had a good life together. Poor Dad, though—he never could figure out how a manufacturer of small appliances managed to sire such a maverick."

"I'm wondering myself," she commented in a low voice.

"It takes one to know one."

"Exactly what do you mean by that?" she said, bristling.

"A rebel, an adventurer, a maverick, a gypsy. I'll bet if you'd been born a boy you'd have stowed away years ago on a freighter bound for Hong Kong." His eyes twinkled at her.

Sinking down in Graham's armchair, Lesley closed her eyes and whispered dreamily, "Tahiti." Realizing what she was admitting, she clamped her mouth shut. But it was too late.

Thane chuckled.

"All right, so I've always wanted to see Tahiti. That doesn't prove anything."

He leaned forward and rested his elbows on his knees. "I can prove it, Les. Remember when we got out of the plane at the ranch and you looked around?" He didn't wait for her answer before he went on softly, "I saw your eyes. You looked as though you'd landed in heaven."

"Anyone would have," she defended herself.

"Sure—anyone would go hunting for unicorns—and Harry will serve frozen dinners tomorrow night."

"You're the one who went unicorn hunting," Lesley reminded him, laughing.

He stood up and walked toward her. His voice was so low she barely heard his words. "And you're the one it came to, Les."

"Don't, Thane," she pleaded. "I . . . I just can't take any more tonight." She dropped her gaze to her book she still held in her hand. He made an impatient sound in his throat.

"Your way this time, Les, but you have to grow up sometime. You can't chase unicorns forever."

"There's nothing wrong with dreams!" she shouted. Tears filled her eyes.

"Dreams can be lonely company on a cold mountain night!" he snapped back.

"I have no intention of being alone forever—but that is none of your business." She faced him defiantly, tossing the forgotten book down on Graham's leather chair with a smack.

"I ought to put you over my knee!" he thundered at her.

"You wouldn't dare!" she screamed.

"Wouldn't I?"

"You bully!"

"Immature little . . ."

"Stop it, both of you!" Harriet shouted from the doorway. The two of them halted in mid-shout.

"Some of us around here are tired and might like to get a bit of rest," Harriet said acidly. "Now, both of you, go to bed!" She stalked down the hall, muttering to herself. Not until they heard her door downstairs slam shut did they move.

Finally Thane said, "Leave it to Harry to have the right idea. Let's go to bed."

"I am not going anywhere with you, least of all to . . ."

His harsh voice stopped her renewed argument. "Forget it, Les. I have no desire to share a bed with you—at least not in your present mood."

Lesley gasped. With no further word, she ran out of the room and up the stairs. To her dismay, he was right behind her. She stopped and turned a flushed, challenging face to him. "Why are you still here?"

"Your graciousness overwhelms me." He grinned. "Graham asked me to stay here for as long as he was in the hospital."

"I don't need you."

Exasperated, Thane took her arm and pulled her toward her room. Pushing her inside, he turned her into his arms. Just before his lips claimed hers, he whispered, "You don't need me, Les? Well, I think that's debatable."

Again, she had no defense against his kiss. Clinging to his shoulders, pressing herself to him, Lesley put the full force of her fear and loneliness—fear for Graham, loneliness at not seeing this maddening man for three days—into her response. Within seconds she was pliant flame in his arms.

Abruptly, he put her from him and held her at arm's length. Staring into her darkened blue eyes, he seemed about to speak, but instead spun around and left the room, closing the door firmly behind him.

Putting her hands to her face, Lesley let the

tears—of fear, of frustration, of hopeless love
—so long denied find their agonizing release.

Exhausted from the hospital vigil and her
crying, Lesley slept almost until lunchtime.
She woke with a throbbing headache and
shadows under her eyes.

The ever diplomatic Harriet exclaimed,
"Ach! You look worse than you did last night,"
when Lesley stumbled into the kitchen.

"Just some juice and toast, Harry, please,"
Lesley said, collapsing onto a kitchen stool.

"Mr. Thane told me to tell you not to come to
work today. He said everything's under control."

"I'll just bet it is," she grumbled. Thane was
now totally in charge of the Institute. The
board members had been delighted to hand
everything over to him, at Graham's grateful recommendation. Although Lesley grudgingly admitted Thane's qualifications, it was
disgusting to her to see how casually, even
enthusiastically, everyone put things under
his domination. Well, not me, she told herself.

"I think I'll go to the office anyway," she
said.

"Miss Lesley! That's crazy. Won't you be
wantin' to see your uncle today?" Harriet
argued.

Lesley closed her eyes and rubbed her tem-
ples. "Yes, of course. Maybe . . . maybe I'll
put off the office for another day." After all,

she'd canceled her appointments anyway, believing she'd be in the mountains all this week.

Harriet shook her head.

Lesley went back to her room, took some aspirins, and dozed for a while, waking to find her headache almost gone. Sighing, she dressed as brightly as she could—anything to relieve the monotony of the sterile white hospital room—choosing a light blue dress patterned with tiny spring flowers. Its wide blue patent leather belt showed off her tiny waist. Paired with matching summer high-heeled sandals, the outfit had always been one of Graham's favorites.

"You look like a little bit of spring," he would say when she wore it.

Before leaving the room, she searched through her bureau drawers for the blue turban-style hat she'd bought once as a lark and piled her hair under it. That, and the use of a bit more makeup than usual, becomingly overcame the ravages of the past few days.

"Graham, I believe you can think about going home," Dr. Bailey announced triumphantly.

To his surprise, no elation greeted his statement. "Please, Gordon, I'm in no hurry."

"You're in no danger, Graham. I understand how you might be, oh, afraid of leaving here—that's just natural—but . . ."

"That's not it," Graham sighed. "I suppose

I'll have to explain, Gordon. You see, as long as I'm here, my second-in-command is at my place, watching over my niece. Now, those two are just right for each other, but you've never seen two more stubborn people. They need a little time." Graham sighed again. "You know, I've been lying here contemplating my own mortality, Gordon. Don't try to placate me, now—I know very well I'm not going to live forever. And my Lesley—she would be totally alone in the world. But with a man like Thane Fraser . . . well, if my illness can bring them together, so much the better."

Dr. Bailey looked into the twinkling blue eyes, alight with mischief. He shook his head. "Graham Chadwick, fairy godfather—I can't quite picture you in that role. Well, I could tell you it's none of your business, but it wouldn't do any good."

Graham shook his head.

"All right, Graham. I will keep the news of your miraculous recovery a deep dark secret. I certainly hope you know what you're doing," the doctor added softly just as Lesley entered the room.

"Hello, Uncle Graham, Dr. Bailey," she said, maintaining the smile she wore for their benefit.

"Well, well, here's the breath of spring I prescribed for you, Graham."

Lesley looked about her with interest at the flowered wallpaper and other homelike accoutrements. "I notice you also prescribed a release from the cardiac care unit, doctor. It was a nice surprise."

Graham shot him a warning look.

"Un, yes," the doctor stammered. "He's doing, uh, well—but we still have to watch him carefully, of course."

Puzzled, Lesley looked from one to the other. "Of course," she repeated after him.

Dr. Bailey peered intently at Graham's chart for a moment, then abruptly muttered something Lesley didn't quite hear and left the room. Lesley went over to the bed and kissed her favorite patient. Plumping his pillow, she asked, "What got into him this morning?"

"Dr. Bailey? I can't imagine. Some personal problem, I suppose. He did seem distracted, didn't he?"

"Oh, well. No matter. You look much better, Uncle Graham."

He smiled at her a trifle sadly. "It will take time, dear," he said softly.

A worried frown replaced Lesley's smile. She squeezed his hand. "And I'll be with you. Don't worry. With Harry's help we'll manage beautifully. The men are coming in a few days to install the chair elevator to your room."

"All this fuss—that's just what I was afraid of, Lesley. It would be a strain on me if a young, healthy woman like you were to burden herself tending to an invalid." He shook his head helplessly.

"An invalid! No, Uncle Graham. Dr. Bailey said . . ."

Closing his eyes, he sighed. "One just never knows, dear."

"Never mind," Lesley ordered briskly. She pulled a chair to the bed and sat down close beside him. "I'm not going anywhere."

"But it's not fair to you—or to Thane."

"What are you talking about?" she asked.

Graham looked at her. Confusion showed in his eyes. "Surely the two of you have come to a decision?"

Sorely tempted to tell him exactly how she and Thane felt about one another, Lesley remained silent and dropped curling dark lashes over troubled blue eyes.

"Oh, children, children," Graham lamented, a ghost of a smile playing on his mouth. "Don't waste time playing games. Believe me, life is too, too short, so humor me."

His reference to the brevity of life sent a pain twisting in her heart. "Anything, Uncle Graham, anything. Just tell me what you want."

Graham patted her hand. "Come, come, Lesley. You must know by now that my fondest wish is to see you taken care of. And nothing would accomplish that better than if you were married to Thane."

Lesley stared at him, her eyes wide with disbelief.

"I'm sorry that you're being cheated of the

ups and downs of a proper, private courtship, but I may not have much time, and . . ."

"Uncle Graham, there's been no . . . I mean, we haven't . . . no mention of marriage . . ." she finally managed to choke out. At least that was true.

Graham smiled confidently. "You wouldn't go off alone with a man you didn't trust and care for."

Horrified at that logic—for it was too close to the truth—Lesley tried to explain. "We were to be an advance party for a later expedition, Uncle Graham. We're . . . we're professionals!"

Her cheeks felt hot as she chided herself, remembering their first morning alone. It seemed centuries ago now, but she recalled every detail. Their actions had scarcely been those of platonic business partners! But that was something Uncle Graham must never know.

"Nevertheless, dear," he was saying, "the fact remains that you are a woman and Thane is a man."

"Yes, but . . ." Lesley could see that further explanation was useless. Though scrupulously fair in dealings with female employees, Graham obviously reverted to traditional attitudes where she was concerned. She decided to try a different tack, make him see the impossibility of his dream. "But marriage . . ."

He interrupted her. "That's where the two of you are headed, whether you know it or not. All I'm asking is that you sacrifice the fuss and nonsense to please a bothersome old man. Too much to ask, Lesley dear?"

He stared at her, but still he got no answer. "I know!" he shouted, making himself cough. He waved away her attempts to offer him some water. Hoarsely, he continued, "I've gone about it all backward. Yes, I shall speak to Thane. This afternoon, when he visits."

"No!" Lesley screamed, then quieted as she recalled where she was. "Not that! Please, Uncle Graham—you must promise me not to mention a word of this to Thane." She managed a light laugh. "These are liberated times, dear uncle. Or do you think I'm too unattractive to get a man on my own?"

"Then you'll do it—you'll make my fondest wish come true?"

Lesley searched the dear face, animated by his dream. But is it impossible? she asked herself. Thane had shown time and again that he was attracted to her, and he, too, owed Graham Chadwick a great deal. Finding an increasingly agitated pair of blue eyes riveted to her face, she sighed deeply.

"Yes, Uncle Graham, whatever you wish." Graham's beaming smile was her reward.

In a daze, she spent the next hour hearing about "dear, dear, Lydia." Finally, she kissed him good-bye, leaving him a new mystery novel to fill the afternoon with until Lydia's visit. Unfortunately, her own distractions were less successful. She spent the rest of the afternoon dreading the inevitable confrontation that would follow her rash promise.

Chapter Nine

Just before dinnertime Lesley entered the town house. Harriet called up from the kitchen, "Miss Lesley, is that you?"

"Yes, Harry. I'll be right down to help."

"Don't bother. It's just one o' them quiches you like so much. Mr. Thane called—there was some emergency or other at work, so he won't be in till late."

"Oh," she whispered, releasing a sigh over the reprieve she hadn't expected. She felt as though she'd been holding her breath for a long time.

With renewed energy Lesley straightened her shoulders and dashed up the stairs, took a quick shower, and came back down in faded blue jeans and a purple T-shirt with the words

JOIN THE UNICORN . . . SEEK THE DREAM printed under the Unicorn Society's prancing
snow-white namesake.

"May I eat with you in the kitchen, Harry?"
she asked.

"Since when have I ever refused you,
missy?" Harriet asked, slicing a loaf of freshly
baked bread. Its irresistible perfume restored
Lesley's flagging appetite. Lesley smiled.
Later she must face her problem; for now,
Harriet's straightforward company was just
what she needed.

The two of them ate together sitting on
stools at the kitchen counter. They talked of
one thing and another for over two hours.
Finally, Harriet yawned and eased herself off
the high stool. Picking up her coffee cup to
carry it to the sink, she said, "It's time I
joined Johnny Carson. Tonight he's got that
scientist fellow who tells about the stars and
all—Hagen?"

"Sagan, Harry—Dr. Carl Sagan, the astron-
omer."

"That'd be him. Reminds me a mite of a
young Mr. Graham, bless his heart. We can
watch together if you'd like," Harriet offered.

"Any other time I would, Harry, but . . . but
not tonight." She managed to smile. "Good
night."

"You get some rest now, Miss Lesley," Harriet said as she went into her own room.

Lesley slowly picked up her own cup and
carried it to rest beside Harriet's. Absently,

she rinsed them both, watching the water flow over her hand. She let her mind wander back to a place of beauty, a place too briefly seen, a place of sparkling streams and snow-crowned mountains, of lakes like jewels. Life was so beautiful, so simple there.

Shaking her head, she turned out the lights and made her way up the stairs, counting each step as she went. Anything, anything to keep her mind off what lay ahead.

The hours passed. She was lying in bed, wide awake, when she heard Thane come up the stairs. Soon afterward the ship's clock in Graham's study chimed twice.

Lesley listened as Thane entered his room, showered in the bathroom they shared, and, presumably, went to bed. For just a moment she considered postponing this confrontation until morning but dismissed the idea. If she didn't discuss it with Thane, she knew her uncle would. That would be more humiliation than she could bear. At least this way she stood a chance of retaining some semblance of dignity in the midst of madness.

To collect her wits she went softly downstairs, brewed a large cup of coffee, and made a sandwich with Harry's leftover meatloaf. She placed the offering on a tray and went back upstairs. Once she almost tripped on the long folds of her white cotton robe. Smothering an exclamation, she went to his door and knocked.

"Thane?" she called softly.

"Come in."

With shaking hand she opened the door. He was in bed with one small lamp burning. To her consternation, he was sitting up reading, with the brown-and-white-striped sheet pulled almost to his waist.

Silence stretched between them, broken only by the steady ticking of his alarm clock. Even the otherwise well-traveled street outside was quiet. Finally Lesley spoke.

"Please, Thane, I have to talk to you." She came close to the bed and put the tray down on the nightstand.

"You will excuse me for not getting up?" he drawled. In spite of herself, Lesley's eyes ran the length of him, outlined under the thin covering, then looked away. She nodded, swallowed convulsively, felt the sharp, familiar pain deep inside.

He sighed. "All right, now what? Today has been one crisis after another." He dropped the papers he was holding and started to rub his neck, knotted with the day's tension.

Lesley stepped closer, drawn by the urge to touch him, then moved his hand and began massaging the tired muscles. He made a satisfied sound deep in his throat.

After long moments during which her massage became slower, gentler, allowing her to enjoy the feel of his warm skin under her fingers, Thane grabbed her hands and pulled her back in front of him.

"This isn't wise, you know," he said.

Suddenly he seemed angry. "What in hell *do* you want, Les?"

Pulling away from him, she stood shakily, her hands held out to him in an unconsciously pleading gesture. "It's not me, it's . . . oh . . ." Unable to stand the tension anymore, Lesley blurted out, "Uncle Graham wants us to be married."

"I know." His voice was quiet, calm.

"You knew! You knew!" she screamed incredulously. She tried to move away from him, but he pulled her toward him.

As if he were explaining rainbows to a child, he said slowly, "Look, Les, Graham treasures you and the Institute. He trusts me to run the place, so naturally it would please him to have me in his family. And naturally his illness would increase his concern for your future. It's a logical mating."

"We're not breeding stock!" Somehow when her uncle had presented his case it hadn't seemed so cold-blooded.

"He doesn't mean it like that, and you know it," Thane said. He gently released her to take a sip of the coffee. "Anyway," he continued, "what does his notion have to do with the royal treatment?" He raised the mug to her in a mocking toast.

Turning from him, Lesley said, in a voice so low he could barely hear her, "I think we should make his dream come true."

"Go on."

"Do I have to say it?"

"Yes."

He was enjoying this! She choked out, "I want you to marry me!" Fleetingly, she wondered if a less romantic proposal had ever been made.

"To please Graham?" he inquired with all the feeling he might use to ask about the weather.

"We owe it to him!" she shouted. "What other reason could there be?" Never, she thought, never must he know that I've been insane enough to fall in love with him!

"Oh, I can think of one," he said softly, replacing the mug on the tray. He reached out a hand and smoothed it over the curve of her breast. Her thin robe and nightgown couldn't hide her instantaneous response.

Gasping, she jerked away.

"No! It . . . it wouldn't be a real marriage . . . we, we wouldn't share a room. It would just be until Uncle Graham is fully recovered. Then a quiet annulment."

Thane smiled into her eyes. "No."

Lesley couldn't believe she'd heard correctly. "No! You'd refuse him this?"

"I'd do anything for Graham, but I won't live a lie for you."

"What do you mean?" she asked.

"A real marriage, Les—same room, same bed." His voice was low but adamant. Her breathing stopped, then began again with alarming harshness.

"No. I can't—I've never . . ."

Thane smiled. His even white teeth gleamed in his tanned face. "I'm well aware that you haven't," he said slowly, causing her pale cheeks to bloom with rosy color. "But I think you *can*. In fact, you show great promise, as I recall."

She couldn't look at him. "Please, Thane," she begged.

"What's it to be, Les? A real marriage or no marriage?" He pulled her close and stared into her eyes.

"What about the annulment, Thane? Why not . . . why not simply get engaged?"

He shook his head. "The shock of a breakup in either case would devastate Graham and hurt my mother, too."

She hung her head, her hair falling forward over her cheeks. "I just don't know."

His grip tightened, hurting her arms. Lifting her chin, he forced her to look into his glittering eyes. "There's someone else? Trevor Saunders, Ben Adams?"

The absurdity of the statement almost made her laugh. "Of course not. My life has been at Unicorn and with Uncle Graham. I didn't want to get involved with anyone for a long time."

"Sorry to upset your plans," he apologized, but his voice held no hint of remorse. "Will you do this for Graham?"

Startled, Lesley just stared at him. When

she'd come in, it was to ask Thane to do this favor for Graham. How had things gotten turned around? "I'd do anything for him. But this! I feel as though I'm selling myself."

Thane sucked in his breath audibly. "If you're selling yourself—good cause or not—what does that make me?"

Lesley shrugged. She had no answer for him.

Thane's grip tightened further. "I don't want a human sacrifice for a bride."

"I'm not a martyr," she insisted, "but I'd do anything for Uncle Graham."

"*Anything?*"

Lesley managed to twist away. Rubbing her sore arms, she shouted, "Yes! Even be a human sacrifice, as you so gallantly put it."

"Maybe it won't be so bad, Les. We're pretty sure we'll be compatible."

Her cheeks flamed. "I've been treated to a demonstration of your expertise, Thane—no doubt gathered after much experience."

"Les . . ."

"I don't want to be one of a cast of thousands."

"You give me too much credit," he said, grinning.

Lesley threw him a furious look. He sobered. "Just keep thinking of Graham," he reminded her. "He *is* the reason for all this, isn't he?"

"Of course!"

Suddenly his good humor—and his patience —evaporated. "It will work out, Les," he said briskly. "Let's just get on with it. All things considered, it makes sense."

Lesley's cheeks flamed anew. Afraid of what she might say, she kept her thoughts to herself. Thane had won again! Terrified as she was by the outcome of their conversation, she couldn't deny a certain elation, too.

Thane stretched lazily in his bed. "Well, I just accepted your proposal. Aren't you going to kiss me?"

A shrill scream of total exasperation was her answer. Lesley wrenched away from him and fairly flew out the door to the accompaniment of his laughter. She slammed it behind her with all her angry strength, then followed suit with her own door.

Three floors below, the unaccustomed noise woke Harriet. She smiled to herself as she turned over to go back to sleep. "I knew from the first night those two would make sparks fly," she murmured. "I'm no Dr. Sagan, but I could see this comet coming."

The next day Thane went into the office early, leaving Lesley to make her own way in. She was relieved beyond words that she didn't have to face him. It wasn't until lunchtime that he sauntered into her office, commandeering her hour off to have lunch with him. Leaving the restaurant, he drove her to Dr.

Bailey's office. At her questioning look, he smiled. "Blood tests."

Lesley submitted to the technician, but she refused to look at Thane just as carefully as she averted her eyes from the needle.

The next day their lunchtime was spent at the courthouse, where Thane presented the blood test results and paid for the license. Lesley signed where she was told; otherwise she remained aloof from the proceedings.

Two uneventful days passed during which Lesley relaxed somewhat. Thane spent almost every waking moment at the Institute; she kept up a schedule of work, mostly at home and with a rapidly improving Graham, now home and beginning to take an interest in the office again. Thus far she had managed only to hint that she and Thane were seriously involved without having to commit herself to her uncle.

The second evening Thane walked in, looking tired and worn, just as she was going up to bed.

"Good night, Thane," she murmured, brushing past him.

His arm shot out, and he pulled her close to be soundly kissed. Utilizing all her self-control, Lesley managed not to respond—too much.

When he released her, he breathed, "Very nice. I needed that."

"You look tired," she remarked. She dug her

nails into her palms to keep from reaching up to smooth his dark, wavy hair.

Glittering dark eyes captured hers. "Care to do anything about it?" His tone was softly insinuating.

Lesley jerked away. His infuriating laughter followed her up the stairs.

Chapter Ten

To her surprise, Lesley slept serenely that night. In the morning she woke irrationally optimistic and lighthearted. She showered, then dressed in her brightest summer outfit, a pink linen suit with a frilly white blouse. It was dressier than her usual office attire, but it seemed right on this bright and shiny day. She was humming jauntily as she went down the stairs. "Top o' the mornin', Harry!" Her greeting stopped abruptly when she discovered Thane already seated at the counter. He rose, smiling.

"Good morning, Lesley," he said, pulling a stool for her next to his. He leaned over and kissed her cheek.

Harriet grinned.

Lesley remained silent, afraid to trust herself to say anything. If she were as cheerful as she had to admit she felt, it would betray too much to Thane. If she were as upset as she'd like Thane to believe she was, then Harriet would never accept the news of their engagement when they announced it. What a tangled web! she thought.

Thane and Lesley left the house together, common sense dictating that she ride to work with him. During the trip she glanced at him. He, too, it seemed, had taken special care with his clothes today. She noticed he had on a dark brown three-piece summer suit with a dazzlingly white silk shirt and richly patterned tie. Round gold and amber cuff links added an extra touch of elegance.

Noticing her gaze on him, Thane said, "Anyone would think the two of us were celebrating something today."

"I am. Uncle Graham is doing well and it's . . . it's a beautiful day."

"Ah, Lesley—so nonchalant about becoming engaged?"

"I never take business arrangements too seriously—it's bad for the nerves," she replied firmly.

The car had stopped for a red light. Thane grabbed her wrist, pulled her clenched hand to his lips. "Take this one seriously, Lesley, or you'll regret it."

A horn sounded behind them. Releasing her, Thane resumed his driving and made the rest of the trip in silence. Lesley's thoughts careened wildly inside her head. Regret it?

What could he mean? How will I survive this marriage? What will become of me? Of us?

By the time they arrived at the Institute, Thane was once again his casual, charming self. He insisted on taking her for a small tour to acquaint her with a number of changes he'd made. Baffled by his swift shifts of mood, Lesley went unprotestingly.

It wasn't long before she was caught up in the new spirit in the various departments, especially the huge photography studios, darkrooms, and film-editing studios, where Thane had hired a new department head. Some innovative equipment for underwater work had just arrived in Ben Adams's domain.

"It's the best in the world, Lesley!" Ben Adams practically crowed, leading her from one highly technical piece of machinery to another. Lesley smiled and nodded, but she was really feigning interest this morning.

Ben had always been an enthusiastic sort, and normally she would have been involved with his explanations, but aware of Thane's suspicions concerning her feelings for Ben, Lesley remained cool toward the photographer. Fortunately, Ben didn't seem to notice as he demonstrated yet another camera. Finally Thane called a halt.

"Excuse us, Ben, but we have to get upstairs. Mrs. Crandall is probably sending out the bloodhounds."

"See you later, Ben!" Lesley called as they

left. This remark earned her a critical glance from Thane. Ben, however, was so absorbed that he didn't even acknowledge their going.

In the elevator Thane asked, "Well, Les, what do you think?"

"Very interesting," she replied coolly. "Does Uncle Graham know about all of it?"

Thane's eyes narrowed. "Don't you mean, does Graham approve? As a matter of fact, he does. I gave him a brief outline of my plans before we left for the Sawtooths, and he gave me carte blanche."

Lesley frowned. Did Uncle Graham know Thane would take his beloved Institute away from him? Despite her undoubted love for Thane, she couldn't let him hurt her uncle, for there was where her loyalty lay.

"Say it, Les," Thane growled.

Startled, she turned to him, but just then the elevator arrived at the office floor. Merely nodding to Mrs. Crandall, who tried to hand him a sheaf of messages, Thane ushered Lesley into his office and slammed the door. Standing with fists on his hips, he waited.

"It's . . . it's just that since you came, you've taken control. Uncle Graham . . ." she stammered. She had to be businesslike about this.

"I would never do anything to hurt Graham," he stated flatly.

Lesley looked down. "I . . . I never said you would."

"That's something," he said. "Shall we get to work?" he added more briskly.

Lesley turned slowly and walked out, past a puzzled Mrs. Crandall, and into her office. Sighing, she sorted through the morning mail, grateful for anything that would take her mind off the questions which filled her head.

She had the pile down to a fraction of what it had been just as Thane sauntered in, unannounced, and said lightly, "It's nearly one, Les. I've come to invite you to a lunch and to a wedding."

The dark head bent over the mail snapped up. Lesley choked out, "A . . . a wedding . . . today?"

"Can you think of anything better to do on a beautiful summer day?" He grinned at her.

"No! I can't! I mean . . . not today."

"Now, is that the proper Unicorn spirit? Of course you can."

"Uncle Graham is expecting me this afternoon and . . ." she argued.

He waved aside her objections. "Call him. I happen to know my mother is there today, so he won't be alone."

To Lesley it was as though he'd said that Graham didn't really need her.

"We're leaving right now, Les. I've already informed Mrs. Crandall. We're going to Judge Barker's chambers and getting married. Somewhere along the way we'll stop for lunch. It's now or never."

Resisting the overwhelming impulse to choose the "never," Lesley conceded defeat. She stood up and removed her purse from her desk. She took her light suit jacket from the coat rack. All the time, she never looked at him.

Thane reached out and pulled her small, unresisting form close. He ran a hand over her hair. Putting a finger under her chin, he tipped her face up toward his. "What's wrong? Don't you want any lunch?"

Lost in his smile, in the dark depths of his eyes, Lesley whispered, "I think I've lost my appetite." He couldn't ignore the invitation of her gently parted lips. "Funny," he breathed against her ear, "mine is increasing."

With a gasp, she pulled away, and with his help forced shaking arms into her jacket. Then she stood, head held high, at the door waiting for him. "Aren't you going to call Graham?" he reminded her.

Lesley stalked to her desk and dialed the hospital. Lydia answered.

"He's gone for some tests right now, Lesley. I'm sorry."

"Oh, well, that's all right. Please, just tell him I won't be able to see him until later than usual today."

"Yes, I know," Lydia answered, then said good-bye.

It wasn't until they were standing in front of the judge that Lesley thought to wonder how

Lydia knew, but by then it was too late. She was already married to the tall, handsome man at her side.

When he bent to kiss her at the end of the short ceremony, she forced her mouth to remain cool and unresponsive under the familiar fire of his kiss. Drawing away, he arched a mocking brow. It's no use, he seemed to say. You can't resist for long. With all the strength in her slight frame she determined to show him just how mistaken he was.

On the drive back, Lesley couldn't help admiring the small gold band she now wore. It was delicately carved and set with tiny chips of diamonds here and there.

"It was my grandmother's," Thane informed her. "Her name was Celine LeBeau Emory—my mother's mother."

"She must have had small hands, too. It fits perfectly." She held it up to the light, where the diamonds winked at her when they caught the sun.

"She did. I remember her quite well—tiny, queenly, French—and a spitfire, just like you."

"If I'm so horrid, why did you agree to marry me?"

"For Graham, remember?" he replied. "Besides, my mother always taught me never to refuse a lady in need."

She determinedly ignored his double entendre. Covering her left hand with her right, she sat watching the sunshine glinting off the city's expanses of glass and the occasional flower boxes on the sidewalks. "Do we have to go to the hospital now?" The thought of announcing their marriage, accepting congratulations, all the fuss over them was just more than she wanted to face.

He pulled into a narrow parking space. "I thought it would be best to let my mother and Graham know, but you could persuade me to put it off in favor of . . . other pursuits." His hand took hers and brought it to his mouth, where he leisurely kissed each finger in turn, sending delicious, dangerous thrills through her.

Inwardly melting but outwardly unmoved by his actions, Lesley said firmly, "Shall we go in?"

"You can't escape me forever, Les."

Hurriedly, she pushed open her door, got out of the car, and started walking away. If he only knew, she thought miserably. I'm on his side, but I can't let him know it!

In seconds he caught up with her and said very low, for her ears alone, "For their sake, Les, at least *try* to look happy."

She stopped. "Do you really think I'm that cruel, Thane? After all this, Uncle Graham will never know from me what a travesty this is." Before he could answer her, she stood on tiptoe, pulled his frowning face down to hers, and kissed him softly. Then she took his arm and walked close beside him.

* * *

"Why, Lesley, how lovely you look!" Graham exclaimed.

Kissing him, Lesley smiled shyly. "Thank you. And how are you today?"

"Never mind me—what's . . ." Graham began, but a quietly smiling Lydia interrupted him.

"He's doing very, very well, Lesley. But I think Thane has something to tell us just now."

Thane held out his hand, and Lesley slowly walked to him. Holding her close to his side, he announced, "We wanted you both to be the first to know. Lesley and I were married just this afternoon." He leaned down and brushed a kiss on her hot cheek.

Lydia jumped up to hug them both. "Welcome to the family, Lesley. I'm so pleased, for both of you."

Graham held out his arms to Lesley. He was elated, glowing, wiping a tear from his eye— Just the way I should look, Lesley thought ruefully. Guiltily she accepted his expressions of congratulations and affection.

If only it were a real marriage, she thought. Then, when she caught Thane's devouring gaze on her, she reminded herself that it would indeed be a real marriage. Her cheeks flamed.

They stayed awhile. Thane astounded Lesley with how smoothly he was able to take odd moments in their embattled relationship and embroider them into the fabric of a courtship, and a romantic one at that. Naturally, he omitted their more intimate moments—at no time, in fact, did he become uncomfortably personal. It was a sterling performance.

Somewhat overwhelmed, Lesley obeyed when Thane decided it was time to leave. She kissed her uncle and was once again hugged by Lydia, who whispered, "I think my son is very, very lucky." They left the hospital room to the older couple, who were holding hands and congratulating each other on the fine pair their "children" made.

As soon as they were out of sight, Lesley removed her arm from Thane's. Pointedly she moved away from him.

"You're quite a storyteller, Thane. You should have been a writer, or an actor," Lesley observed.

"Stories?" he repeated in mock affront. "Did I say anything that wasn't true?"

Lesley shrugged uncomfortably. "No, not exactly, but . . . you know what I mean. It was the way you presented it."

Thane helped her into the car. Frustrated, she grabbed the car door and slammed it before he could close it. Grinning, he got in and drove them to Graham's house, where they were greeted by a wildly fussing Harriet.

Embracing Lesley, she exclaimed, "Such news! And the two of you, keeping secrets from poor old Harriet! Congratulations!"

"Harry, how did you find out?" Lesley said. "Uncle Graham?"

"Don't you think it was a kindness for somebody to tell me?" Harriet stepped back, wiped her eyes, and blew her nose loudly into a neatly pressed handkerchief.

Thane kissed her cheek. "You'd have been the second—no, third—to know, Harry, right after Graham and my mother. Honest."

Placated, Harriet walked back to the stairs, indicating two battered suitcases as she went. "I'll be leaving just as soon as I get a proper dinner finished."

Lesley's shout halted her. "Leaving!"

"Don't worry—it's just for a week, to give you a decent honeymoon. Besides, my sister, the one in Brooklyn who runs the catering service, well, she needs some help, this bein' the busy time of year for weddins' and all." Starting down the stairs, she went on, "There's plenty o' food—as if you'll care a tiddle for that!" She laughed at her own joke.

Lesley ran to the stairs, and leaned over the wooden railing. "Oh, Harry, please don't . . ."

Thane was there before she could finish, grabbing her arm to quiet her. "What Les means is that it's very considerate of you, Harry." He was rewarded with a furious look from Lesley. "Ah-ah, my love," he whispered, "remember, you're a happy bride."

Twisting away from him, Lesley walked stiffly up the stairs to her room—anywhere to get away from the mocking gaze in those dark eyes. Once there, she stripped off the pink suit she had donned in such a happy spirit this morning. She found her oldest, most faded, and most comfortable robe, put it on, and lay down on her bed.

She was scarcely relaxed when her door opened and Thane walked in as casually as if he'd been doing so for years. Indignant, she sat up. Suddenly remembering their changed status, she closed her mouth before she said anything. He looked so handsome! He'd discarded his jacket, tie, and vest. The silk shirt was partly unbuttoned, and the way it emphasized his muscled tanned chest did funny things to Lesley's breathing.

He looked around the room slowly, touched the childhood mementos, the few dolls and stuffed animals she'd saved, and then walked to her desk, where she kept pictures of herself with her parents. "You have your father's dark hair and your mother's eyes. Graham's too. They're the first thing I noticed about you—those big, incredibly blue eyes," he said softly.

"Dad always said that even though he didn't have much money, he would always possess the most precious sapphires in the world, as long as he had Mom and me," Lesley told him. "She missed him so much."

"And you?"

"Of course—he was a wonderful father. But for Mom—well, they were special—together," she answered. Then, without thinking, she added, "It's what I always planned for when I marr—oh!" Her hand flew to her mouth.

There was a pause. Slowly, she raised her eyes to his. "I'm sorry, Thane . . . I—I didn't think."

To her surprise, he smiled. "Not thinking, Les, is what you do best." He walked toward the door. "Harry sent me to tell you dinner is almost ready. I'll wait for you downstairs."

Lesley stood uncertainly for a while, then went to her closet. Sorting through her clothes, she finally chose a long, flowing caftan of Moorish pattern in shades of musky rose and glittering gold. She had bought it for a special party Graham had given at the house a few months before. It was rather daring, with a plunging neckline that revealed the soft curve of her breasts but otherwise covered her from shoulder to tips of fingers and toes.

There, she thought, looking in her mirror. This looks right for a wedding night. The thought was nearly enough to change her mind about the outfit. She put her hair up in a loose bun, letting stray wispy curls drift over her neck and cheeks. As a last gesture of bravado, she dabbed her best, most exotic perfume behind her ears, between her breasts, and on her wrists. Two deep breaths, and she started down the stairs.

Chapter Eleven

Harriet waited at the bottom of the second flight. Her eyes widened when she saw Lesley. "How lovely you are, girl," she said, hugging her. "Now," she continued, after wiping at her eyes, "dinner is ready, so serve yourselves. My cab is waiting. Good-bye, Miss Lesley. You be happy now."

Grabbing a suitcase in each hand, Harriet let herself out to Lesley's, "Bye, Harry, and thank you!"

Thane came up behind her.

"Beautiful, Les," he said, causing her heart to pound alarmingly with the knowledge that they were alone.

Turning slowly, she tilted her head slightly, accepting his compliment in silence. He took her hand and led her into the dining room, where Harriet had spared no effort to set a beautiful table.

"Oh, Harry," she breathed.

Thane laughed. "I always knew she was a romantic at heart."

"But where did she ever get fresh flowers at this hour?" Lesley wondered aloud, touching the delicate bouquet that graced the center of the small round table.

"I asked her the same thing. Harry, it seems, has no end of talents, including brow-beating reluctant tradesmen. In no uncertain terms she informed the florist that if he ever wished to do business with Mr. Graham Chadwick of the Unicorn Society Institute again, he had better have a suitable flower arrangement at this address posthaste."

"Leave it to Harry!" Lesley laughed.

"Let's not let her efforts go to waste," he prompted. He held her chair out for her. She slid into it. Bending over her, he inhaled deeply. "Mmm. Les, whatever perfume you're wearing could convince me to let Harry's 'proper' dinner get very, very cold."

Lighting the candles in their branched silver holder, Thane took his seat. He uncovered the steaming bowls of buttered noodles and asparagus, and served them each a plateful. Offering him a roll from the napkin-covered basket, Lesley smiled. She fought to keep her lips from trembling.

Their gazes locked—his steady and glittering, hers uncertain, even pleading, though she knew not for what.

Desperate to end the moment, Lesley whispered hoarsely, "We'd better eat our dinner, Thane, or it'll be ruined."

He smiled. "Such a practical wife!"

They ate in silence.

Thane offered her some wine. Hoping it would give her a bit of courage, however false, Lesley held up her glass. Sipping it, she noticed his glass was empty. "Would you care for another kind?" she asked, half-rising to fetch another bottle from Graham's extensive cellar. The wines were Graham's one extravagance, and he was very proud of them.

Thane shook his head. "I've never developed a taste for spirits. Haven't you noticed?"

Thinking back over the many times they'd dined together—each crystal clear in her memory—Lesley realized she'd never seen him drink anything but mineral water, fruit juice, and occasionally, coffee. Not for anything would she let him know how indelibly each moment with him was etched in her heart. She merely shrugged.

When they finished, Thane said, "Harry told us to check the kitchen when we were done—for more instructions, no doubt." He started to get up, but Lesley waved him back down.

"I'll check," she insisted, disappearing through the door and down the stairs in a drift of sparkling silky folds. Thane's gaze followed her. When she was out of sight, he closed his eyes, took a deep breath and ran agitated fingers through thick dark waves. By the time Lesley's voice sounded on the other side of the door, he'd composed himself again.

"Are you ready for this?" she called gaily. The door opened; she entered carrying a small layer cake decorated with pink flowers and presided over by a tiny bride and groom. With a flourish, she set it down on the table.

Thane regarded it a moment. "So Harry's talents extend to bakers, too."

Laughing, Lesley sat down. "Obviously."

"Isn't there some ceremony or other surrounding the cutting of one of these?" Thane asked.

"It's not important, really."

"Look, Les, between your uncle and me, you've been cheated out of all the traditional trappings. If custom says we're to eat that cake while perched on the spire of the Empire State Building and whistling 'Dixie,' then call a cab and start whistling."

Lesley laughed. "I can't whistle."

"I'll teach you," he said. "Now, are we going to eat that cake or not?"

She looked down at it. "It seems a shame to cut it, but all right. I think it's done like this," she said, picking up the knife and taking his hand, somehow ignoring the electric shock she felt at his touch. "The first piece we cut together, and feed some to each other."

He smiled into her eyes as his hand over her small one pressed the knife into the cake. He picked up a bite-sized piece and waited for her to do the same. In the manner of all brides and grooms, more cake went into their laps than into their mouths, but they laughed at their attempts to satisfy custom. Lesley felt some of the tension recede.

Thane retrieved some of the larger crumbs, and dropped them on the lace tablecloth. "Now are we allowed a real slice?"

Nodding, Lesley brushed crumbs off her dress. "Go ahead. I really couldn't eat another thing. Why don't I make some coffee while I clear away the dinner things?"

"No thanks—too warm. But I'll help you— see what a good husband I am?"

For just a second the word *husband* took her aback, but then she retorted, "Doing your share won't win you any medals from me, Thane Fraser."

"Ouch!" he cried in mock injury. "Prickly, aren't we?"

"Just reasonable."

He grinned at her, but he didn't argue further. He stacked the dishes in the dishwasher while Lesley put away the leftovers.

"Nothing left to do, Les—in here," he said softly.

Breathlessly, she turned to face him. Her eyes were enormous in her pale face and her mouth trembled noticeably.

He pulled her easily into the living room. There he pushed her down on the couch. He stood, dark and compelling, above her in the dim light.

"Really, Les, I'm not going to beat you!"

"I . . . I know," she choked out. All the tension she'd felt earlier returned full force. She couldn't bring herself to tell him that the love she felt for him made him immeasurably important to her, so important that she was frozen with fear.

With a groan, he threw himself beside her and took her in his arms. Probing, plundering, his mouth seared hers until she sighed his name. She offered no resistance as he traced a burning trail across her cheeks, down the simple column of her throat.

Without conscious effort, they found themselves stretched full length, side by side on the soft cushions. Lesley could feel the straining of his body toward hers, seeking the fulfillment of their passion. Her senses responded with an answering need. His hands stroked over her back, finding the zipper of her dress, easing it down until his fingers had free rein to explore her warm, smooth skin from neck to waist.

"Les, let me love you," Thane was whispering in her ear, calling her back with a jolt from whatever lands her desire for him was leading her to.

Love! There was no love in this marriage, in this passion—not on his side! Pushing him away with all her strength, she screamed, "No! Let me go, Thane. No!"

After what seemed an eternity, his arms slackened around her. He sat up. With a pang, she saw that she'd unbuttoned his shirt completely during those tumultuous moments in his arms. Elbows resting on his knees, head supported by his hands, he muttered hoarsely, "Get out, Lesley, before I do something that will make you hate me even more."

Lesley scrambled up. She clutched her dress up over her breasts. "Please, Thane, I don't . . ."

"Get out!" he shouted.

"I'm s-sorry," she whispered before she turned and fled upstairs.

Two miserable, endless hours of tossing and turning later, Lesley heard Thane's measured tread on the stairs. She held her breath until his footsteps passed her door and entered his own room. She stared at the ceiling, unable to forgive herself for her behavior downstairs. The dress, the perfume, the dinner, her initial passionate response, then her seemingly quixotic withdrawal would have been unforgivable in a casual acquaintance; in a wife—even one whose marriage wasn't based on mutual affection—such actions were appalling.

She tried to sleep, but every time she closed her eyes, all she saw was a picture of how he'd looked in his bed the night she'd proposed this insane marriage to him. And she saw his face, strained with the control he'd exerted downstairs, his tanned skin pulled tautly over high cheekbones and firm jaw, his tantalizingly mobile mouth gone straight and cold.

She rose and walked silently out of her room, not stopping to put a robe over her clinging, pale yellow nightgown. She was well aware it revealed more than it covered, but she no longer cared. A strange mood, rooted in her unrequited love, possessed her. She didn't stop to question her actions.

Quietly, she opened his door without knocking. The room was nearly dark. Clad only in the short robe, Thane was standing by the window, one hand holding back the drape to allow the cool breeze to blow in. To her surprise, the other hand held a drink—a bottle of brandy stood on the dresser beside the window.

"What do you want?" he asked, startling her. He remained standing at the window, staring out into the electric glow of the city night.

Lesley fought a sudden impulse to run. "I . . . I don't know. I couldn't sleep."

"Well, I don't know any lullabies."

Ignoring his sarcasm, she asked softly, "Why are you drinking? You said you didn't . . ."

His harsh voice interrupted her. "I detest the stuff. But it's helping."

"Helping?" she repeated blankly, moving closer.

Thane dropped the drape and spun around. He stared at her, his eyes moving over her slowly, examining every inch of her. Somehow she stood quietly. He raked his fingers through his hair.

"I see." She felt frightened, confused, elated, aching with want of him. Still, she couldn't bring herself to let him know, to take the final, irreversible step.

"No, you don't see. Don't you have any idea of what you do to me?"

Lesley shook her head. Her hair fell forward over her cheeks. In seconds gentle hands were there, pushing it back over her shoulders. Then gentle arms held her close. Lesley felt him tremble; or maybe it was her body. She couldn't tell.

"I think I could use a drink, too," she whispered against the thunder of his heartbeats beneath her cheek.

"Why would you want a . . . oh, Les!"

Eager lips raised to meet his.

Into the hush after the storm Thane whispered, "Are you all right, Les?"

She drifted in a sensual daze, trying to come back to earth. Lesley nodded against his chest. She felt his arms hold her tighter.

"Sleep now," he murmured against her hair, kissing her brow, her eyes.

Lesley was sure she was too keyed up to rest, but she closed her eyes obediently and fell at once into a deep, peaceful slumber.

Some hours later a loud crack of thunder awakened her abruptly. "Thane," she murmured, reaching a tentative hand to touch his cheek. She had to convince herself that he was real, that what they'd shared had really happened.

He captured and kissed her hand and then her wrist. As he bent to find her lips, he pulled her arm around his neck. The soft touch of his mouth and the hard feel of his body against her nakedness ignited glorious fires within her and melted her bones. She arched against him, offering herself to his molding touch. Her response was total, overwhelming. Once again, they explored worlds closed to field teams and expeditions—for only lovers may journey in these magic kingdoms.

This time Lesley had no doubts or questions. She loved Thane. Surely his reckless passion proved that he had some feelings for her. Her head pillowed on his chest, she smiled before sleep once again claimed them both. The storm without proceeded until dawn, but they never heard it.

She awakened slowly. Surveying the room in daylight, Lesley spied an alarm clock on the bedside table. It was past ten. Yawning, she turned to greet Thane and chide him for being so lazy. Her heart filled to bursting with the sweet knowledge of the change in their relationship. Now all would be well—she was positive—and if he chose to stay in bed a little longer this morning, she knew she would agree wholeheartedly.

He wasn't there.

Chapter Twelve

Frowning, Leslie sat up in bed. "He's probably downstairs," she told herself aloud. Pushing back the sheet, she stood up, retrieving her nightgown from where Thane had tossed it on the floor the night before. After a quick shower, she pulled on a robe and went downstairs, her step light as her heart.

A quick search of the rooms, and both her step and her heart became heavy with nameless dread. How could he leave her, today of all days? She sat down by the phone in the den a moment, then dialed the Institute.

"Mrs. Crandall, it's Lesley—may I speak to Thane, please?"

"Miss Wall—I mean, Mrs. Fraser! We're all so thrilled, and we wish you so much happiness. Why . . . ." she gushed.

"Yes, thank you, Mrs. Crandall. May I speak to, uh, *Mr.* Fraser?" Lesley tried her best to remain formal and businesslike, but being called "Mrs. Fraser" nearly proved her undoing.

"Oh, dear," Mrs. Crandall said, obviously flustered. Lesley thought ruefully that since Thane's return the unflappable Hester Crandall had been coming unglued with alarming frequency. "He's not here, Mrs. Fraser. He left a note on your desk—he said he knew you'd be coming in later. Something came up—in the field I think—"

Lesley interrupted her. "I see. I'll be in as soon as possible." Without waiting for a reply, Lesley hung up the phone, buried her face in her hands, and let the tears come. *Something came up!* To leave her so casually after last night was unforgivable! In her heartbreak all professional concern for the Institute left her. All she could think of was the lovemaking they'd shared. She had given all she could give; in her inexperience she thought he'd done the same. "What a fool I've been!" she cried.

She sat there, staring about her as if she'd never seen Uncle Graham's den before. The phone rang. Reluctantly, she answered it, hoping and fearing it was Thane.

"Hello," she said quietly.

"Lesley, dear, it's Lydia. Thane called me before he left. I'm so sorry, but, well, it couldn't be helped. Are you all right there alone?"

The warmth and caring in her voice tore at Lesley. How she wanted to confide in that kindness, receive reassurance and comfort. But she was married now—she wouldn't go crawling off for sympathy.

"Good morning, Lydia. I just woke up, but I'm fine. Mrs. Crandall at the Institute told me he had gone."

"That boy!" Lydia clucked. Lesley had to smile. Only his mother could even remotely consider the man she'd married a "boy." "I told him it was horribly inconsiderate not to wake you and tell you, but you know how he is. He didn't want to worry you."

"Really, it'll be all right, Lydia," Lesley reassured her. It will be all right, she told herself, because I'll make it all right.

"If you say so, dear. Now, Thane said he'd leave you a note at the office, though I think it's scandalous that either of you should work today. And he left me instructions, too. May I meet you for lunch, Lesley?"

Unable to think of an excuse to refuse, she acquiesced.

"Oh, Mrs. Fraser, I'm so happy for you, so very happy."

Lesley leaned over the desk and kissed a cool, well-scrubbed cheek. "Thank you, Mrs. Crandall. I appreciate it." Earning a tremulous smile, Lesley went into her office where she found a single long-stemmed rose and a note propped against her antique brass inkwell. It said:

Les,
  You looked so peaceful lying there I didn't have the heart to wake you when Mrs. Crandall called. The team in the Everglades ran into major problems—I had to go—you understand. I'll be traveling into the swamp, so I don't know when I'll be able to call. **Should** be back within three days. I called my mother—she'll fill you in on some other plans.
  We'll talk when I get back.

Miss me,
T.

Sitting down, Lesley smoothed it out on her desk blotter and read it again and again. Desperately, she searched each word for some sign of love or affection. How could he? Last night no words had been exchanged; they had spoken with their hands, their lips, their bodies. This morning she needed more. Naturally, she had assumed he would tell her he cared. Now it seemed to her that he had wanted her, used her, then had found it a simple matter to walk—no, to fly—away from her. Hurt beyond words, she stood up, paced around her small office. "Miss me." That was the problem—she would miss him, as surely as the sun rose. But if it took every bit of strength she possessed, he would never know how much.

171

Following a totally unproductive morning, Lesley welcomed Lydia at the small, bustling restaurant. Seated at the small round marble table, they each ordered a salad and tea.

Lesley was startled to hear Lydia say, "Your apartment is all ready for you. It's been quite a mess these past few days, but I think that you'll be pleased with the results."

"Apartment? What apartment?"

"Honestly, that son of mine can be impossible sometimes," Lydia sighed. "Thane's apartment, Lesley. He's had it since long before he returned to Canada to get things right in Fraser Enterprises. He was staying at Graham's just until it could be cleaned and remodeled. I've been there since I came back to New York."

"Why was he still staying at Uncle Graham's?"

"Your uncle asked him to—and I suppose there were other attractions," Lydia replied pointedly. "Anyway, he's arranged for movers to come for your things tomorrow."

"But Lydia, where will you go?"

Coloring slightly, Lydia told her, "Well, Graham has asked me to stay at his home—while he recuperates. Harriet will be our chaperon once he's home, of course. Graham seems to make a habit of taking in Frasers."

Realizing that she was lovingly but firmly being pushed out of the nest, Lesley accepted the inevitable. It was obvious that Graham was still in love with Lydia—and the feeling appeared to be mutual. She couldn't help feeling it would be disruptive and inconsiderate of her to intrude.

"Where is my new home?" she inquired lightly. She hoped she didn't sound as breathless as she felt.

Lydia named an address even more prestigious than Graham's. Lesley's eyes widened and the older woman looked at her sharply. "Thane never mentioned that he's quite wealthy?"

Lesley shook her head. "He told me he was the son of a manufacturer of small appliances."

Lydia laughed. "Small appliances, tools, sporting equipment, textiles, and a few other things—I never can remember them all. Thane diversified, or subsidized, or one of those things corporations are always doing. At any rate, somebody else runs things now, thank heavens."

Lesley tried to smile, but she was too amazed by Thane's status. What other surprises were in store, she wondered. "I . . . I see," she managed to whisper.

Lydia patted her hand sympathetically. "You probably don't. I never did. My André always said he kept me around solely for decorative purposes. As for my son's habits— well, I'm still trying to understand him."

Smiling, Lesley said, "I'm sure you were a wonderful mother. And I know you meant much more than that to your husband."

"Perhaps. He was a fine man, much like Graham, but without that reckless spirit of adventure." Lydia stirred her tea and considered Lesley a moment. "You know, dear, somehow I think you won't be content with the role I chose."

"I intend to stay with the Institute. We quarreled about that once, but I think Thane realizes now that I won't be a stay-at-home, pampered doll."

"Looking at you, I can understand why he felt that way at first," Lydia observed. "But I think he's very happy that you are the way you are." After a while, she checked her watch. "Oh, it's time I was at the hospital. I'll call you or your secretary—Mrs. Crandall?—about the movers and all. What little I have with me they'll take to Graham's when they pick up your things. Take care, dear."

As they parted on the busy street, Lydia kissed her cheek. "I'm going to like having a daughter." With a jaunty wave, she hailed a cab and was gone.

Lesley stood lost in thought, until the doorman at the restaurant tapped her shoulder. "Is everything all right, miss?"

She smiled brilliantly at him. "Mrs.," she corrected him softly, walking off in the direction of the Institute.

Lesley loved the apartment at first glance. Colorful Oriental rugs covered parts of the gleaming wood floors, and much of the furniture was antique; yet those pieces were smoothly integrated with modern, low, sweeping couches and a variety of sculpture and other art from pre-Columbian artifacts to prints and collages by modern masters. It had some of the same elegance as Graham's home, but with more of a contemporary feel to it. Everywhere she saw evidence of his strong personality.

Lesley especially enjoyed the spacious kitchen with its glazed red tile floor and lavish use of copper and wood in its accessories. Her favorite haven immediately became the book-filled library, which was furnished with brown leather chairs and contained a small oak library table, obviously antique, which Lesley used as her desk.

The second evening, as she was sorting through books in the library finding places for her volumes on the shelves, the doorman called, announcing a visitor. She frowned at her disreputable cuffed jeans and Unicorn T-shirt and waited for the doorbell to ring. Expecting Lydia, Lesley smiled as she opened the door, only to find herself greeting a stranger. The woman was tall and startlingly beautiful—honey-blond hair and green eyes. Her extraordinary figure was set off by what was obviously a designer dress.

Lesley gestured her in. The woman strode past her, looked impatiently around the apartment with an air of familiarity. "Where is Mr. Fraser? We had an appointment for this afternoon."

"May I ask who's calling?"

"I'm Della. Just a moment—who are you?"

Della! Lesley swallowed nervously. "I'm Mrs. Fraser. Would you care to sit down? Perhaps I can help."

Della sank gracefully onto the nearest chair. "Thane's *wife*? He never told me . . ."

"It was all rather sudden."

"I see. Well, congratulations. I hope you'll be very happy."

"Thank you."

"I hate to disturb you, but might I see Thane?"

"He's not here right now. There was an emergency on one of the expeditions, and . . ."

Della rose, walked to the door. "Say no more," she said. "I understand. Just ask him to contact me whenever he returns from the wilderness." Before she left, she turned back to Lesley with a friendly smile. "I hope we'll meet again soon. Good-bye."

When she'd gone, Lesley closed the door, locked it, and spent a long, miserable evening wondering why Thane had chosen her over the ravishing Della. Grudgingly, she admitted the woman was not only lovely but seemed to be a nice person, too. Surely, she told herself, Thane wouldn't marry me, just to please Graham. Thane was far too independent to be coerced into such a situation, wasn't he? Sighing, she went to bed, knowing the questions could be answered by only one person, and he was far, far away—from her voice, from her sight, and from her empty, empty arms.

Lesley dashed past Mrs. Crandall with a hurried, "'Morning. Would you bring me Uncle Graham's dictaphone—I'll have some letters ready for you by lunch, if I'm lucky!"

Once in her office, she'd scarcely put her purse down when a voice behind her said, "If honeymooners can be late, I'll have to give it a try."

"Trevor!" Lesley squealed. For there he was, lanky and grinning, lounging on a chair.

He rose, came toward her, and gave her a hug. Stepping back, he took her left hand in his and examined her wedding band. "Nice, really nice. But no surprise."

"What! How . . . where did you come from?"

"I was in the city on business, so I thought I'd drop by and check on the two of you. That nice lady out there"—he cocked his head toward the outer office—"remembered me from a couple of years ago and filled me in on your big news. By the way, I'm also glad to hear your uncle's doing okay now."

"Thank you. But I still don't understand why you're not surprised."

"Anyone but a blind man—or woman—

could see how you and Thane felt about each other."

Lesley groaned. "Was I that transparent?"

"You both were—to everybody but each other." He grew serious and said softly, "While I'm on the subject, I'm sorry I . . . uh . . . barged in on you that morning up on the mountain."

Lesley felt her cheeks grow warm. "Please, don't worry about it. I'm . . . I'm grateful you were able to find us."

"No problem—we always camp there the first day out. Now tell me, when did that mule-headed idiot see the light and marry you?"

Suddenly the tension of the past few days caught up with her. With tears threatening, she walked into his willing, if confused embrace. "We were married about eighteen hours before he left on a troubleshooting trip for the Institute." She snuggled closer, welcoming Trevor's uncomplicated, brotherly affection.

"He's a bigger fool than I thought."

"Not anymore," said a cold, flat voice from the doorway.

Like guilty lovers, Trevor and Lesley stepped away from each other. "Hold on, Thane, you don't believe that Lesley and I . . ." Looking at Thane's face, Trevor realized his words were futile. He glanced at Lesley. "I'll go now, Lesley. If you need me . . ."

"She won't," Thane grated out. He stepped aside. Trevor walked out, muttering to Thane as he went, "By the way, congratulations. Don't go messing up the best thing that's ever happened to you."

Giving no indication of having heard him, Thane closed the door and stared at a pale and shaking Lesley.

"Thane, you don't understand . . ." How could she tell him Trevor was comforting her bruised emotions, bruised by him because she loved him so much? Her only choice was the truth, though she'd sworn she'd never admit her love. Such oaths, she thought miserably, were always doomed to be broken.

"Thane, we were—Trevor was sorry for me. I was so lonely, so un . . . unhappy without . . . that is, when you left, and it's been days, and when he came, it . . . it was like having a little of you here, and . . ." She trailed off, hating herself for her incoherency.

"Go on," he prompted, though there was no warmth and less encouragement in his tone.

Her eyes raised to his; she forced herself to step closer and touch his arm. "I love you, Thane."

For just a moment something passed across his face, but it was gone as swiftly as it came.

"The worse for you," he said softly as he closed the door behind him.

Chapter Thirteen

Sore in spirit, Lesley stood for a long time beneath the shower's stinging spray. She tried in vain to send her tension down the drain with the soapsuds, but she could not forget the stricken expression on Thane's face when he had stormed out of her office that afternoon. Sighing, she turned off the water and reached around the curtain for her towel. When she couldn't find it, she leaned out of the tub and to her surprise found Thane leaning against the door.

"Is this what you are looking for?" he asked, handing her the towel.

"Thane! Please!" She snatched it from his hands.

Beneath hooded lids he watched her as she

wound it around her sarong style and stepped carefully out of the steaming tub.

She noticed that his hair was still damp from a recent shower and that he was dressed in a fresh shirt and business suit. "Are we going somewhere?" she asked.

He shook his head, then stepped forward to place his hands on her bare, wet shoulders. "No. We're not. I am."

"You can't! Not now!"

"Can't?" He raised an eyebrow. "Do you really think you could stop me?" His voice was quiet. "Besides, I won't be gone long. I am just going to think things out. When I have a problem, I have to find my answers alone . . . by myself." He smiled faintly, then looked at her sharply. "Do you understand?"

"I'm trying to, but I'm frightened, Thane." She lowered her eyes. "May I come, too?" He would never know what it cost her to ask. It was the final triumph of her love over her pride.

"Not this time, Les . . ." He lifted her chin and gazed into the blue depths of her eyes.

"Thane," she began, "about Trevor, and us . . ."

"Forget it, Les. Again, I went a little crazy— or a lot crazy. Trev will understand. Maybe too well," he added ruefully.

"And us?" she prompted, her heart beating wildly.

"I promise you, Les—everything will be

straightened out soon. I just want to breathe free again."

"Without me," she whispered. She knew he'd heard her, but he didn't reply. Terrified she already knew what his answer would be, Lesley fell silent.

Thane tugged her towel away and held her close and for a long moment, his hands enjoying her soft fragrant warmth. Bending low, he pressed a kiss on one breast and then the other before he kissed her long and full on the lips. Her arms twined around his neck, desperately holding him, but he gently pushed her away and held both her hands cupped in his.

"Take care, Lesley."

Then he was gone, leaving her once more alone.

Like a robot, Lesley prepared a meal, but she couldn't eat it. It was all too incredible: Thane, finding her in Trevor's arms, innocent though the embrace was; Thane, angry and passionate; Thane, distant, saying good-bye.

"Too many good-byes," she whispered, wiping at her tears.

She lay awake for long hours, hoping against hope that he would return, come back to her arms. Finally, she slept. In the morning there were shadows around her eyes, and her face in the mirror looked back at her pale and lifeless.

She made excuses not to see Graham. Her

uncle was a perceptive man. Not even skillful makeup would cover the misery in her eyes, she knew. By phone, Lydia assured her that she needn't worry—Graham was improving by leaps and bounds. He would probably be home any day. Lesley tried to take some comfort in the fact that her marriage had done her uncle, at least, some good.

Harriet called the second day of Thane's absence. The beloved housekeeper was just the medicine Lesley needed. A little later, Trevor phoned.

"Are you, you all right, Lesley? Did you make your thickheaded husband see some sense?"

Somehow she laughed. "Don't worry about it, Trev. When are you leaving town?"

"So anxious to be rid of me? If I'm that dangerous, I'm flattered!"

"About as dangerous as a beagle puppy, and you know it," she retorted.

He hesitated. "How is Thane?"

"Thane . . . Thane isn't here right now, Trev."

"I don't believe it. He left you again on some harebrained expedition?"

"Not . . . not exactly."

There was a long pause. "Because of me, in the office? Les . . ."

"No, Trev. I'm sure Thane realizes his accusations are absurd. I can't explain him. Please don't ask."

* * *

"Enough is enough!" Lydia exclaimed. "My son has gone too far! It's one thing to run around the planet for the good of the world when he's single, but he has responsibilities now!" She looked indignantly at Lesley, who was sitting listlessly on the couch one late afternoon several days after Thane's abrupt departure. Lesley opened her mouth to remonstrate but was unable to get in a word. "That boy! Ever since I can remember, whenever he has something on his mind he runs off somewhere alone to some impossible spot! Is that any comfort to you, my dear?"

"You don't know how much," Lesley assured her. "Did I tell you he's at the Saunders' ranch? Trevor called as soon as he got back and saw Thane." She paused and avoided her mother-in-law's eyes. "Lydia, would you tell me about Della?"

"Della Hagerstrom?"

Lesley frowned. Surely there couldn't be two Dellas in Thane's life? "I think Jason Saunders said Della Harrington."

"The same. She's a relative—by marriage. She was a Harrington, from Philadelphia, but I think she lives in New York now."

"She's divorced?"

"Why, no, dear. We were invited to the wedding about two years ago. She married a . . . an attorney, that was it. I believe she has a baby girl, in fact. Yes, definitely, she does live in New York. Why, Lesley?"

Lesley fought to keep her voice normal. "She stopped by here looking for Thane while he was gone."

"Come to think of it," Lydia mused, tapping a forefinger on her cheek, "yes, Thane did mention her to me. She's an investment analyst, you know, and she often contacted André for advice. She's probably asking Thane now —they always were great friends."

"Just . . . *friends*?"

"Of course. Once Della asked Thane to take her camping at the Saunders ranch, but it was a disaster. They all laughed about it. Della decided that she was a city girl after all!" Lydia paused a moment and looked at Lesley. "My son is a maddeningly private person, but this I do know—he has only been in love once. He married the girl."

It took a bit of cajoling to convince the pilot of the small plane to fly Lesley to the ranch at dawn, but nothing was going to stand in her way now that she'd decided to take matters into her own hands. As the plane lost altitude before landing, Lesley peered anxiously down. Trevor had delivered her message to Thane! Her heart lifted when she saw the tall figure standing beside his horse, his hand shielding his eyes against the rising sun.

Not a word was exchanged as he helped her mount the extra horse. Once they reached the familiar campsite, Lesley simply walked into his outstretched arms. "Thane, my darling," she sighed against his lips.

Smiling in triumph, Thane scooped her up and bore her to the sleeping bags, zipped together. "Sorry there's no convenient threshold. Will this do?"

For answer Lesley tightened her arms around his neck.

Much, much later, Lesley asked softly, pressing her warm, silky skin against Thane's muscled leanness, "Do you think Uncle Graham will have the good sense to follow our example?"

"As a matter of fact," Thane answered, twining a strand of her fine hair around his finger, "he called me last night to tell me his roving days were over."

"A logical mating," she said demurely.

Thane laughed aloud. "We know those are the very best," he exulted before his lips found hers again.

Catching her breath, Lesley sighed. "Let's go farther into these mountains, away from everything."

Thane rubbed his hand over her bare hip, causing delicious thrills to course through her. She snuggled closer as he said, "Dear love, if I had my way, I'd take you to the far side of the moon."

"The Sawtooths will do," she insisted, pressing a gentle kiss to the strong brown column of his throat.

"Well," he drawled, "they did pretty well once."

"I suppose we'll have to go back to work sometime," she observed, purposely changing the subject.

"The Unicorn Society Institute awaits. But Graham insisted we have at least a week's honeymoon. Then it's back to the city."

"I hope you don't have to go off too much, like that trip to the Everglades."

"Those situations don't come up very often. I've had my share of adventures. Now life and a home with you are what I want."

Unable to resist teasing him, she traced his lips with her finger and said, "I was looking forward to some adventures of my own."

"Far be it from me to stop you. Mind if I come along—and bring the kids?"

Lesley smiled. "Oh, Thane, I'm so happy. I never want this moment to end."

Thane looked thoughtful. "Someone once said that happiness is a process, not a place or a single time. All that matters, my love, is that we're on the right path, and no matter what, we're together."

"Together," Lesley echoed before his lips claimed hers, "on the trail of the unicorn."

Genuine Silhouette
sterling silver bookmark
for only $15.95!

What a beautiful way to hold your place in your current romance! This genuine sterling silver bookmark, with the distinctive Silhouette symbol in elegant black, measures 1½″ long and 1″ wide. It makes a beautiful gift for yourself, and for every romantic you know! And, at only $15.95 each, including all postage and handling charges, you'll want to order several now, while supplies last.

Send your name and address with check or money order for $15.95 per bookmark ordered to

Simon & Schuster Enterprises
120 Brighton Rd., P.O. Box 5020
Clifton, N.J. 07012
Attn: Bookmark

Bookmarks can be ordered pre-paid only. No charges will be accepted. Please allow 4-6 weeks for delivery.

N.Y. State Residents
Please Add Sales Tax

Silhouette *Romance*

IT'S YOUR OWN SPECIAL TIME

Contemporary romances for today's women.
Each month, six very special love stories will be yours
from SILHOUETTE. Look for them wherever books are sold
or order now from the coupon below.

$1.50 each

Hampson	☐ 1 ☐ 4 ☐ 16 ☐ 27 ☐ 28 ☐ 52 ☐ 94	Browning	☐ 12 ☐ 38 ☐ 53 ☐ 73 ☐ 93
Stanford	☐ 6 ☐ 25 ☐ 35 ☐ 46 ☐ 58 ☐ 88	Michaels	☐ 15 ☐ 32 ☐ 61 ☐ 87
		John	☐ 17 ☐ 34 ☐ 57 ☐ 85
Hastings	☐ 13 ☐ 26	Beckman	☐ 8 ☐ 37 ☐ 54 ☐ 96
Vitek	☐ 33 ☐ 47 ☐ 84	Wisdom	☐ 49 ☐ 95
Wildman	☐ 29 ☐ 48	Halston	☐ 62 ☐ 83

☐ 5 Goforth	☐ 22 Stephens	☐ 50 Scott	☐ 81 Roberts
☐ 7 Lewis	☐ 23 Edwards	☐ 55 Ladame	☐ 82 Dailey
☐ 9 Wilson	☐ 24 Healy	☐ 56 Trent	☐ 86 Adams
☐ 10 Caine	☐ 30 Dixon	☐ 59 Vernon	☐ 89 James
☐ 11 Vernon	☐ 31 Halldorson	☐ 60 Hill	☐ 90 Major
☐ 14 Oliver	☐ 36 McKay	☐ 63 Brent	☐ 92 McKay
☐ 19 Thornton	☐ 39 Sinclair	☐ 71 Ripy	☐ 97 Clay
☐ 20 Fulford	☐ 43 Robb	☐ 76 Hardy	☐ 98 St. George
☐ 21 Richards	☐ 45 Carroll	☐ 78 Oliver	☐ 99 Camp

$1.75 each

Stanford	☐ 100 ☐ 112 ☐ 131	Browning	☐ 113 ☐ 142 ☐ 164 ☐ 172 ☐ 191
Hardy	☐ 101 ☐ 130 ☐ 184	Michaels	☐ 114 ☐ 146
Cork	☐ 103 ☐ 148 ☐ 188	Beckman	☐ 124 ☐ 154 ☐ 179
Vitek	☐ 104 ☐ 139 ☐ 157 ☐ 176	Roberts	☐ 127 ☐ 143 ☐ 163 ☐ 180 ☐ 199
Dailey	☐ 106 ☐ 118 ☐ 153 ☐ 177 ☐ 195	Trent	☐ 110 ☐ 161 ☐ 193
Bright	☐ 107 ☐ 125	Wisdom	☐ 132 ☐ 166
Hampson	☐ 108 ☐ 119 ☐ 128 ☐ 136 ☐ 147 ☐ 151 ☐ 155 ☐ 160 ☐ 178 ☐ 185 ☐ 190 ☐ 196	Hunter	☐ 137 ☐ 167 ☐ 198
		Scott	☐ 117 ☐ 169 ☐ 187
		Sinclair	☐ 123 ☐ 174
		John	☐ 115 ☐ 192

$1.75 each

☐ 102 Hastings	☐ 133 Rowe	☐ 156 Sawyer	☐ 181 Terrill
☐ 105 Eden	☐ 134 Charles	☐ 158 Reynolds	☐ 182 Clay
☐ 109 Vernon	☐ 135 Logan	☐ 159 Tracy	☐ 183 Stanley
☐ 111 South	☐ 138 Wilson	☐ 162 Ashby	☐ 186 Howard
☐ 116 Lindley	☐ 140 Erskine	☐ 165 Young	☐ 189 Stephens
☐ 120 Carroll	☐ 144 Goforth	☐ 168 Carr	☐ 194 Barry
☐ 121 Langan	☐ 145 Hope	☐ 170 Ripy	☐ 197 Summers
☐ 122 Scofield	☐ 149 Saunders	☐ 171 Hill	☐ 200 Lloyd
☐ 126 St.George	☐ 150 Major	☐ 173 Camp	☐ 201 Starr
☐ 129 Converse	☐ 152 Halston	☐ 175 Jarrett	

—#202 DREAMTIME Hampson
—#203 A SECRET VALENTINE Browning
—#204 MIDNIGHT SUN Carroll

—#205 RACE THE TIDE Maxam
—#206 AN ADVENTURE IN LOVE Manning
—#207 MORE PRECIOUS THAN PEARLS Wind

$1.95 each

—#208 SUNSET IN PARADISE Halston
—#209 TRAIL OF THE UNICORN LaDame
—#210 FLIGHT OF FANCY Eden

—#211 GREEK IDYLL Walters
—#212 YESTERDAY'S PROMISE Young
—#213 SEPARATE CABINS Dailey

**Look for _PRACTICAL DREAMER_ by Dixie Browning
available in May and
WESTERN MAN by Janet Dailey in June.**

SILHOUETTE BOOKS, Department SB/1
1230 Avenue of the Americas
New York, NY 10020

Please send me the books I have checked above. I am enclosing
$_____ (please add 50¢ to cover postage and handling. NYS and
NYC residents please add appropriate sales tax). Send check or
money order—no cash or C.O.D.'s please. Allow six weeks for delivery.

NAME_____

ADDRESS_____

CITY_____STATE/ZIP_____

Silhouette Romance

Coming next month from
Silhouette Romances

Love So Rare by Anne Hampson

Dawn had unwillingly married Ralf Deverell, yet as the weeks passed, she realized she had fallen in love—with a husband who wanted to keep their marriage a secret.

Her Mother's Keeper by Nora Roberts

How could anyone fall for the unscrupulous author Luke Powers? Gwen knew that she should persuade him to return to California, only now, he'd be taking her heart with him!

Love's Sweet Music by Jean Saunders

Accompanying pianist Paul Blake on his Continental tour was a dream come true for Angela Raines. Her only fear: he saw her as another easy conquest.

Blue Mist Of Morning by Donna Vitek

Anne Fairchild made it a rule never to get involved with her boss. However, Ty Manning left her little choice and before she knew it, he was commanding her love.

Fountains Of Paradise by Elizabeth Hunter

Jewelry designer Michal Brent went to Sri Lanka to buy unusual and beautiful stones. But the most precious jewel she found was the jade green glance of Hendrik Van de Aa.

Island Spell by Dorothy Cork

Working for author Guy Desailley on his island retreat was no easy task for Aidan Elliot. The attraction was immediate—but could love blossom when they were both so cynical about romance?

Silhouette Desire
15-Day Trial Offer
A new romance series that explores contemporary relationships in exciting detail

Six Silhouette Desire romances, free for 15 days!
We'll send you six new Silhouette Desire romances to look over for 15 days, absolutely free! If you decide not to keep the books, return them and owe nothing.

Six books a month, free home delivery. If you like Silhouette Desire romances as much as we think you will, keep them and return your payment with the invoice. Then we will send you six new books every month to preview, just as soon as they are published. You pay only for the books you decide to keep, and you never pay postage and handling.

 — — — **MAIL TODAY** — — —

Silhouette Desire, Dept. SDSR 7O
120 Brighton Road, Clifton, NJ 07012

Please send me 6 Silhouette Desire romances to keep for 15 days, absolutely free. I understand I am not obligated to join the Silhouette Desire Book Club unless I decide to keep them.

Name_____

Address_____

City_____

State _____ Zip_____

This offer expires October 31, 1983